Jill Eisenstadt's
FROM ROCKAWAY

"A well-crafted . . . first novel. Eisenstadt creates
genuine people and defines a distinctive world."
 —Michiko Kakutani, *The New York Times*

"A smart and snappy first novel . . . Dramatically
satisfying, with little excess and lots of crisp
dialogue."—*Kirkus Reviews*

"An exciting new talent."
 —Guy Lesser, *New York Observer*

"The minutiae of a lifeguard's amiable days are well-
documented, anchoring the book in fresh experience.
. . . Eisenstadt is a thoughtful writer. . . . She shines in
the details."—Paul Rudnick, *Los Angeles Times*

"It races to a tense, compelling climax."
 —Carter Coleman, *Atlanta Journal-Constitution*

FROM

ROCKAWAY

JILL EISENSTADT

VINTAGE
CONTEMPORARIES

VINTAGE BOOKS

A DIVISION OF
RANDOM HOUSE

NEW YORK

Library of Congress Cataloging-in-Publication Data
Eisenstadt, Jill, 1963–
    From Rockaway.
    (Vintage contemporaries)
    I. Title.
[PS3555.I844F7   1987b]   813'.54   87-45947
ISBN 0-394-75761-0 (pbk.)

TO JOE McGINNISS

FROM ROCKAWAY

Prom Night

The limo driver, Russ or Gus, has a bald, tan head and a line of whitish crust on his lip edges. He does not try to hide his disgust—"Kids today." Drives like he's in a bumper car down at Playland, like he's doing some huge favor—"Carting brats around town." And has nothing at all to say besides "When I was your age . . . ," "The world has gone haywire," and "At this rate, you'll be lucky to make twenty intact."

In the backseat, a pile. Limbs and hair, smushed corsages, empty, rattling champagne bottles, and pot seeds. Timmy and Alex, Peg and Chowderhead, having long since tuned out Russ or Gus, discuss who will get the Polaroids afterwards.

The camera does belong to Chowder's mom, but Timmy was acting photographer, Alex is the only one leaving for college, and the pictures star Peg, in that violet chiffon gown, before and after the big tear, when her toe got caught. She somehow forgot to lift the dress; stepped out of the limo and right on through it. One perfectly smooth motion that she then managed to re-enact for the camera, exactly.

The decision about the pictures is made tougher still by the fact that no one cares *that* much (to insist on keeping them) yet everyone cares enough not to drop the subject. A resolution seems impossible until Russ or Gus pipes up and suggests making copies. Copies?! You're a genius, thank you, thank you.

Timmy moves to snap a few shots of the back of the driver's neck, which he's been involuntarily watching for hours now. It is fat and wet and jiggling. It is overflowing out of an incredibly dirty, white starched collar. Timmy is sure it's the place where all the guy's bad shit is concentrated. "I mean, imagine having to carry that around every day. Flesh knapsack."

Alex frowns. "You're talking too loud." Peg. is busy examining her split ends. Chowderhead says it'd be a helluva lot worse to have no neck, like Lefty.

They are zipping down Cross Bay Boulevard. Russ or Gus takes advantage of their attention to launch into yet another sermon on "years ago," as if no one had parents to supply that.

"Years ago, we had proms in gyms. . . ." Racing past THE PORK STORE, TUX TOWN, PIZZA CITY. "We couldn't just go molesting any pretty girl that happened by. We had chaperones." Flying at such a clip that Howard Beach is a glimpse, a smell—air getting fresher, saltier. "Do you know how long I saved up for my prom? Do you know how many floors I washed to buy a corsage?" Into Broad Channel, where people live in the water, in houses on stilts, and where Peg once, during a fight, invented the popular insult "Shut up or I'll untie your house."

"No bozos back then, we were clean. No highfalutin ideas about—"

"Beach!" Chowderhead reminds him as they swerve onto the bridge back toward Rockaway. "We wanna be let out at the beach." That inflexible law stating that each prom night must end with a sunrise.

"Listen, wise guy, I'll stop when I damn well please. *We* were at least taught some respect. *We* knew our place." Becoming totally reckless now, his whole body facing them. Could mean into the bay the hard way.

"I see. Well. May we please, sir, be dropped off at the beach, sir. It seems to be our place, sir." The words made doubly comical by Chowder's flat, pink face. Though sunburnt to shit at the start of every summer, he still can never get that sunscreen thing together, or else he forgets. It's no big deal. Minor, he says, if you consider all the other redhead torments.

There's a wave of nervous giggling. Alex, squirming between Timmy and Peg, drinks the vodka swill straight, thinks, this driver is on the edge of a nervous collapse. She cannot face, Jesus please no, the idea of dying before ever even leaving Rockaway.

It is dark still and sticky. Timmy, with his whole head and half his torso out the window, sees Queens glow far off and, closer, gnats, moths, mosquitoes, flying up to taste the bridge lights. These he prefers to all those unhappy fishermen who stand at the edge of the bridge gawking at the limo. How can they keep going, knowing that if anything's biting (unlikely), it will be too polluted to eat? And insects, they are also definitely superior to the sudden sight of Sloane's bashed-in Dodge Dart following the limo again.

Although Sloane has not attended the prom, he has gathered a crew—Bean, Artie, Lefty, Louie the Lump, and, naturally, Schizo, his lifeguard mutt—to go everywhere the prom-goers go, including the Staten Island ferry, where they got extra obnoxious with that disappearing ink stuff, which, as it turns out, disappears better on some fabrics than others.

But no one else seems quite as bothered by it all as Timmy does. Maybe because he's wearing and worried about Alex's dad's tuxedo, or maybe because he's upset that he won't be graduating, since he, like that car full of dirtbags tailgating them, dropped out a year ago. For no real reason.

Inside the limo, they're still talking "back when." Peg, with her blond, nearly white head in Chowder's lap, goes on and on for the benefit of—who knows? It sounds almost like a rap song.

"I'll bet all those girls at your prom were virgins. I'll bet they drank fruit punch and did all their homework because they had to get ready for church, eat all the food on their plates, brush their hairs one hundred times when they woke up, and when they kissed their mothers in their nightgowns they meant it, and when they said the Pledge of Allegiance to the flag witch's-honor Girl-Scout's-honor cross-my-heart-hope-to-die-stick-a-needle-in-my-eye they meant it, and knew all their multiplication tables without flashcards, backwards and forwards and in French, Spanish, Italian, Swahili. . . . Alex, man, wouldya stop yawning already?"

Alex smiles, though slightly nauseated with the feeling that she has just gotten her period, shit, in her white dress and when she'd begun considering having sex with Timmy tonight. For fun. For old times' sake.

When she'd bought the prom tickets she hadn't known she'd be breaking up with him. She'd never really expected to get into college and especially not with a scholarship. Which just goes to show—never try to assume or predict, things will always happen differently. Even when whatever is gonna happen happens, it will appear to be different from the way it actually is. For instance, Timmy, next to her, with his just-hatched-chick hair, honest brown eyebrows, flair for making anything he wears, even tuxes, look like pajamas. He didn't mean it when he said love. An elaborate fling was what it was; quickly simmering to average, then fair, then habit, then a goddamn drag. Whereas real love would be simple. It might shoot up and down until it spontaneously combusted, but it would not, could not, just dissolve.

This thought makes her want to chew her lip, but she's made a resolution to try not to. It scares her to think that everything ends up divided into Before and After: Before and After school, Timmy, prom night. You can look at the Polaroids that way too—prom night, Before and After it got dark, they got smashed, Peg's big tear, Alex got her period. Like those pictures of people who have lost fifty pounds but are somehow wearing the exact same outfit both times.

It's fine with Timmy that Alex is staring at him, but he wishes she didn't have such a sad mouth on. He could do all kinds of nice things with that mouth if she'd let him. She was probably already forgetting their pact fantasy to be together one day in a bed, like grownups. They had made love only in his showerhouse, in his car, in his backyard. And now no more.

Chowderhead says it is four-thirty. "Time to exit this prom hearse." And they are finally cruising up to the boardwalk, perceptible sighing, they're alive!, scrambling to gather from the seat and the floor what's left to ingest, as Russ or Gus pulls up *onto* the curb to make sure he's sufficiently noticed.

Timmy spots Seaver, the old bum who's their friend, doing wheelchair wheelies by the beach wall. Without a word they all jump out of the limo and run to circle him. They all try to talk to him at once. So much to say—about Manhattan, the way it looked from high up in the Time-Life building, sparkling, the moment when Alicia McHenry's name was drawn randomly for prom queen and she was found passed out in the lobby, the ferry ride, the after-hours blackjack place, and, how could we forget, Russ or Gus, the fearless kamikaze limo driver.

To all this Seaver simply nods. He is a survivor of adventures only rumored because he has no tongue to tell of them himself. He can wheelchair as fast as anyone can run and can throw a wicked screwball, and has fish heads tattooed all up one side of his body. Chowder is trying to show him the Polaroids but it's much too dark, which Seaver manages to get across by shaking his head, by holding the photos up close, then away, then up close.

"OK," Chowder says, "forget exhibit A, check out B," pointing dramatically to the hole in Peg's gown.

Seaver bobs his head around, then wheels over and sticks his hand through, softly squeezes one bony knee. Chowder starts chanting, "Easy access, easy access," and clowning with Peg's dress too. Because it's obvious that Seaver is only being friendly. Because Peg in any dress is a once-in-a-lifetime event.

There's a fire on the beach where all the prom people have silently scheduled to meet. And wouldn't you know, Sloane has screeched up in his Dodge Dart, whooping and bellowing to join in. Following him, his animal, Schizo (ugly mixture of Lab and pointer), yapping like he's been fed speed (likely), and then Bean, Artie, Lefty, Louie the Lump, definitely on the prowl tonight, the excitement of all those rampant necklines.

Timmy vows to himself that he will not allow them to interfere with his good time. He admires the June tan that Alex got special for the white dress, white teeth, soft, small, unbearably lickable shoulders. And she is jumping over the beach wall now, on the sand, bending to remove her stockings slowly, man.

"You're whipped," Chowder says, watching Timmy watch Alex.

Chowder just doesn't understand.

. . .

Peg's pissed. This Russ or Gus guy, paid in full, is *still* sitting there, staring. You'd think he'd be thrilled to leave, the way he bitched. Some sort of weird punishment, is it? And for who—them or him? Or out of gas maybe, bored, lost, tired, psychotic? There is nothing she can see that is particularly fascinating or exotic to look at here.

She tries ignoring him, then throwing shells at the windshield, and, as a last resort, running up and sticking her tongue out. That works. He drives off. Peg removes her shoes to jog after him, shouts, "So long! . . . Let's do it again some time soon! . . . You've been too too wonderful, really great!"—thinking as the car rounds the corner how her father would have taken down the license plate number and filed a complaint.

Chowderhead is massaging Seaver's neck, singing "How's about a date?" to the tune of "Eyes Without a Face." He's known for the amusing way he fucks up songs. Could be that something's really wrong with his hearing, since it's been going on for years now. Back in Catholic school he ended up inventing some truly blasphemous hymns, and Louie the Lump claims that when "Stayin' Alive" first came out he caught Chowder mouthing "Chicken Delight, Chicken Delight" in all seriousness.

Peg whispers Chowder's new mixup to Timmy, and he to Alex, who claps. Timmy watches her move closer to hear more clearly, thinks he can tell exactly how she feels, biting her lip while she leans on the wheelchair arm. She's working on holding the laughter back but it shows, it's all over her face, shiny, anxious, the size of his hand. Oh, Chowder could not possibly understand.

"When's this sunrise supposed to go on?" She scans the beach, which Seaver can't get down onto from the boardwalk unless he's carried. "Dontcha feel like we're in some magazine?" she asks as she pulls over her head one of the stockings she's taken off. "Ya know, on the beach, in formal wear?"

But no, no one does know except Seaver, who immediately makes a noise like a cat scream and begins posing. Classy. Innocent. Sexy. Carefree. Amazing, this drunk, crippled, half-deranged bum giving his impression of glamour.

"When do I get *my* massage?" says Peg. "I'm the one who paid for the prom tickets, tipped the driver, bought the pot, and I don't make nearly as much money as you guys." Which reminds Timmy and Chowderhead simultaneously that they have to go lifeguard in about four hours.

"Boo hoo hoo," Chowder says, because Peg's a lifeguard too and makes plenty. Then he switches to rubbing her neck, much nicer, almost too familiar—rubbed, kissed, hugged by him off and on since Catholic school.

Timmy is telling Seaver about the umbrella girl dancing in the Peppermint Lounge. Red plastic raincoat and nothing, no thing on underneath. Seaver bares what is left of his teeth and gives the thumbs-up sign.

"She was ugly," Alex says. "Cellulite." She remembers that she thinks she's gotten her period and grabs Peg to come for a walk. They're only a little ways onto the beach when Bean runs up, picking his ear and babbling about a parakeet that flew into his window, said, "Good bird, stupid bird," and got sexually excited over the color green. They leave him there still yakking.

By the time they find a safe wall to pee near, there is a crack of light on the horizon, the faintest line, cantaloupe color over the edge of Playland. And no, Alex does not have her period, but Peg does—figures, she always gets hers first, which Alex attributes to Peg's having a stronger personality. Alex wants to ask what to do about Timmy, if it's mean to sleep with him when they've broken up for good. But she only wants Peg to say that she should, so she doesn't ask.

"I guess I gotta go home for a sec," says Peg. "Shit."

But Alex offers her house, it's closer, and, besides, she'd like to take Scrapy, her dog, out for a walk.

So they race. And because Alex knows Peg's faster, she compensates by crashing into her every few paces, their dresses tripping them until they give up, giggling.

"Shhhh," at the back door. "My dad's probably up watering the plants or something."

When they get back the boys are naked. They've gone swimming. Seaver's beginning to doze off, with Alex's father's tuxedo draped over his wheelchair.

"Where've ya been?" in unison, dripping.

Timmy is acutely aware of the limited darkness left. If he doesn't get some action going soon it will be too late, make that too early.

"Let's just say the Good Humor man came." Lame joke from Peg. "Hey, idea. Whataya say we play statues? That's what we used to do waiting for the ice cream truck, remember? Let's play." She tackles Chowderhead, tickles him until he says OK, he'll play, but only if he's allowed to stay naked.

"I forget the rules," Timmy says.

"Fake it."

"My dress," Alex says. "My mother."

"Take it off."

"Any beer left?"

"Yes, yes."

"Well, then, let's go!"

But it's nowhere near as easy as it used to be—leaping around on dry sand in a gown, in the heat, and when you can barely even see your hand in front of you. Trying to stay frozen as one or another ridiculous statue, when all you've been doing for the last ten hours is drinking, Scrapy sniffing at your crotch, and the penalty for moving being three Hail Marys in pig latin. Ailhay Arymay. Ailhay Arymay. Ailhay Arymay.

"I'm not too good at this game," complains Alex, lying down. "Can we please, sir, have a time out now." Sweating, mildly queasy.

Timmy takes this as his cue to lift her up—"Time out! Time out!"—spin her around, around, over his head, running. The sunrise continues as a growing smudge, unimpressive. The party by the fire is going strong, and is a similar smear of dull color quickly gone as Timmy runs on, twirling Alex higher, racing with her up onto the boardwalk and stopping in front of the lifeguard shack, really just a trailer, collapsing. Poor elderly Scrapy, who wanted nothing more than to protect his master, has barely been able to keep up, limps toward them, settles himself into a heap of fur at Timmy's feet. And Alex, for some reason, is breathing the hardest of all three.

She proceeds to tell about how the retriever got his name—from the way his nails scrape on the sidewalk when he's leashed. Timmy can't believe that she'd think he hadn't heard that one, after two years of seeing her, c'mon. She must be way more whacked than she's acting.

He laughs, exposing all those screwed-up bottom teeth, then swears, having kicked the door open wrong, with his bare foot, at a strange angle, hard. Inside, he lays her down on a bench the way he would some drowning victim and he stares down at his injury.

"Lockers!" she squeals. "How romantic!," licking her lips, noticing what a fine statue naked Timmy makes. Big shoulders and skinny legs. His middle toe already swollen and purple. Now he's finding room for himself beside her by lifting her legs onto his lap.

"No fair," Alex says. "Taking advantage of a helpless ex."

"The more helpless, the better," he answers, happily. "That's what I'm trained for, to save you, I can save you." He easily removes the white dress, no protest, touching her breast, she's not even angry, letting him kiss her stomach, which is warm, pale, tasting of baby powder. Her hair on his neck instantly makes him forget about his toe, Sloane, everything. Her breath, even though beer breath, gets him insanely worked up.

But things have begun shooting off in Alex's insides and she's burping. "I feel sick—I'm really sorry but the room's revolving, I feel sick." Which immediately has Timmy on his feet (aaah, the toe) and going to fetch flat Coke, aspirin, washcloth, and a paper bag in case she pukes.

In the few minutes that all this takes, Timmy realizes how concerned he is that Alex is feeling bad, more concerned than bummed that there'll be no sex. And that sucks. Imagine what Chowder would have to say about that, he's beyond whipped, he's got serious problems. Ailhay Arymay.

Alex is wrestling with her wrist corsage. It is cutting off her circulation. She is sure that if she can just get it off she'll feel better, but this turns out not to be the case.

"God," she groans, when Timmy returns. "This was gonna be one of those days of our lives like they have on the Kodak commercials. I'm sorry." Timmy's train of thought follows a direct line from Kodak to Polaroids to camera and, holy shit, he must've left Chowder's mom's camera in the limo.

"Hold on," he tells Alex. "Just relax, I'll be right back." As he covers her with the white dress she says, "I'll never mix again, never," and, "What if I die here before I ever even get to college?"

The shack office, through a door from the locker room, is full of flies and first-aid equipment, crumpled soda cans and paper airplanes. On the walls, surfing champ Mark Richards rides wave after awesome wave and ten or so nude black and Oriental women (the preference of Fleming, the lieutenant) pose for gynecological checkups. The posters have Timmy looking down on his own bare body while listening to a phone ring somewhere in Brooklyn, all uptight about the camera, about Alex, about the borrowed tux. None of it belongs to him. In the dim room, even his own skin seems alien—that lonely erection couldn't be his, hairless chest, no way, monstrous shoulders and overall tan like unwashable dirt. His toe hurts. His whole foot actually, and the other one too, from the dress shoes he's had to wear (still out there with Seaver). The limo people will not pick up.

Alex is asleep. She's breathing noisily, making a sound alarmingly like the one Recessa Annie, that plastic mouth-to-mouth wench, makes. A petal from the corsage is stuck to the skin under one of her arms, which hangs off the bench and doesn't look at all real.

Outside, there's some kind of rumbling going on. Timmy assumes it's the Parks Department trucks coming by to get garbage. But the commotion goes on too long to be that; it's becoming almost frantic. He opens his locker, removes the mildew ball of shirt and shorts inside, and goes out to see what all the racket's for.

Day out. Just like that it's day. The same people still hanging around, but they're jumping up and down on the boardwalk now, shouting, surrounding what must be a fight. Alicia McHenry, rejuvenated prom queen, is standing on Lefty's shoulders, waving her banner wildly. Bets are being made, people shoving to get a better view of dog wound around dog, a moving pretzel—Schizo beating on Scrapy.

Timmy sees blood and right away risks being bit to step

in and break it up. "I cannot believe you people." Not at all fair. Scrapy is so much older, so much nicer, not to mention that he is Alex's.

"You suck," Sloane says. "You're a fuckin drag, ya know that?" He strokes unharmed, slimy black Schizo.

Timmy thinks of asking how the fight started but doesn't really want to know. Scrapy's got a gouge in his neck, a lot of scratches, he's whimpering, he's afraid even of Timmy, who has an extremely difficult time getting him to sit the fuck down.

Louie the Lump, who can once in a while be decent, walks over to tell Timmy that Peg, Seaver, and Chowderhead said to meet them at the diner for breakfast.

Well, now there's the missing tux, camera, sick Alex, sick Scrapy, and a busted toe. Things could not be worse. He's got to lifeguard in an hour and a half with Sloane for a partner, and neither of them has slept. But the diner sounds good. Food. He'll order the Earlybird Special plus bacon plus two scoops of butter pecan ice cream, his favorite.

He drags Scrapy back to the shack and dresses the wounds, not so bad-looking when washed off. Then he tries to wake Alex softly, but she leaps up, backs away from him.

"What happened?" she squeaks.

"A lot." Timmy goes on to explain. But as soon as he gets to the dog part, tears collect and she won't listen to the rest. She insists that they get Scrapy to a vet, quick.

"It's all right," Timmy tells her. "I fixed him up myself." He's hoping for a reward kiss. No go.

He shows her into the shabby office where Scrapy is whining, and then they walk slowly out the door and down the boardwalk toward Alex's house. She does not want breakfast. She wants sunglasses. When they arrive at her street she won't let him walk her up, says thanks, rushes off with an armful of dog. Timmy, watching her deal with and eventually dodge a nosy neighbor mowing the lawn, thinks: A girl in an evening gown marching down the street at seven a.m. with her bleeding pet might seem really funny—if only she weren't Alex.

Since the last thing he wants is to face his mother or, worse, his aunt, Sister Agnes, he runs the whole way to the diner, barefoot. In the parking lot he thinks he sees a limo but tells himself it can't be the same limo and goes inside.

Chowderhead, Seaver, and Peg are in a booth by the window, not saying much. Their eggs look fluorescent.

"So." Timmy sits. "I guess it's over." He gulps someone's sugary, lukewarm coffee dregs.

"Where's Alex?" asks Peg, and without waiting for an answer, "Look over there." She points across the room to where, sure enough, Russ or Gus reads the paper and stuffs his face with pancakes.

"Lucky thing." From Timmy, evoking incredulous stares all around. "I mean, I think I left the camera in the car." He decides to forgo the Earlybird Special for four scoops of butter pecan instead.

"Butta *pee*can?" repeats the waitress, apparently not from Rockaway. "At this time of day? Butta *pee*can? Four scoops of butta *pee*can?"

"Just bring him some goddamn ice cream," Chowder scream-whispers. He cannot bear to hear her say those words again. Even more annoying, she's been calling him "Cheddarhead" all morning. Unclear whether it's his red hair, choice of omelette, or simply that she's eavesdropped wrong.

Peg says Russ-Gus gives her the willies bad. That she's going right over to straighten out the camera thing. Seaver appears to get a kick out of this and Timmy, as usual, is confused, totally.

"Why does she want to talk to him if he spooks her out? I don't get it." He's relieved to see the tux *and* his church shoes on the wheelchair.

"Who knows," shrugs Chowder. "I got a wicked headache."

The waitress slams down the ice cream and asks if there's anything else they'll be needing. She's got this hair—what is it? tawny?—defying gravity, with the texture of insulation.

"Any aspirins?" asks Chowder.

No answer.

"I'll take OJ, large, and an iced coffee, black, please."

To Timmy she at least nods. She adjusts her metallic tube top.

Seaver yawns politely and motions for someone to find him a cigarette. When Chowder stands up, a flood of sand comes out his pants pocket. A definite sign of beach sex, which starts Timmy feeling sorry for himself. If Alex were here she'd order waffles like she always does.

"Get this!" Peg says, returning flushed. "That little lech!" She waits for the waitress to put down Timmy's order and then leave before she continues. "The fucker made a pass at me! He asked me out, can you believe that?"

Seaver nods, sure. Timmy just eyes the guy. When Chowder gets back he can't help cracking up.

"He's a sick man." Peg's shredding her place mat.

"And what about the camera?"

"He doesn't know. He says he'll look. God, he's gross. I think I'm ill."

"Oh no. No more of that." Timmy launches into an elaborate version of Alex and the dogfight.

After breakfast the camera is recovered. Also outside, they

discover six full pails of weakfish. Quite an attraction, being so repulsive and just sitting there all lined up on the black-top like that. Timmy squats to touch one of the eyes. It is filmy cold and reminds him of that children's game where you have to stick your hand in a bag of something disgusting and guess what it is.

THE BLOOD | 1
PART

Once, when Timmy was a baby, his ears bled. At least that's what his mother tells him whenever he gets into trouble. The story's become like one of those poems they force you to learn "by heart" in grammar school. Some poem Timmy can recite perfectly, even now, but which he has never actually thought about.

Bean, Artie, Chowderhead, all his friends have heard about the incident more than once because Timmy often has difficulty remembering whom he tells what. And hearing it for a second, third, fourth time, the story does not change a whole helluva lot. But Timmy's whispered delivery gives them the creeps each time, and enough excitement that they don't interrupt. They like it. It's all very exotic because it takes place in Ohio and because blood is unfailingly fascinating, particularly from the ears, and because none of them has seen a tornado, ever.

Ohio is similarly foreign to Timmy, who, like his friends, grew up in Rockaway, New York. He remembers nothing about the tornado that made his ears bleed but, twenty years later, he knows all the details: how it whipped past the house taking the birdbath with it and three and a half lawn chairs and a statue of a black jockey holding a lantern; and how the sound was, according to his mother, "like I imagine dog whistles would sound if we could hear them."

It is her only story that does not, by now, thoroughly bore Timmy, perhaps owing to the fact that he's always in some mess when he hears it or maybe because, although it is about him, he feels no relation to it.

His mother's so worked up, orange lipstick comes off on her teeth and she looks about to spit. It scares him. The way she's yelling the story at him—having somehow made a connection between the tornado and Timmy being caught by the Coast Guard last night, DWI in a borrowed powerboat—scares him.

They stand in the kitchen on either side of a round Formica table.

"I saw blood on the pillow first," she says, "then some came out of your ear. Dontcha remember, Timothy, a little?" Her voice, competing with "Love Boat" on the TV by the sink, is both controlled and hysterical, depending on what part of the story she's telling. He thinks about mouthing her words the way Chowderhead used to mimic the nuns in grammar school when they got too repetitive, but he doesn't have Chowder's balls.

When his mother asks if he remembers, her voice drops, and he wouldn't even be able to hear her over "Love Boat" if he didn't know exactly what she was going to say. "Dontcha remember, Timothy, a little?"

It pisses her off, he thinks, that I cannot remember her Ohio with the corn and the Tastee Freezes and the lawn furniture, so incredibly still and dark "before that tornado," she says. "Afterwards I screamed for Jesus so loud the neighbors came round to ask after me. And the neighbors weren't two feet away like here." The bullfrogs and the outdoor grills, maybe even the Cincinnati Reds, Timmy thinks, all of it reminds her of something about me that just pisses her off.

Looking up, Timmy sees some very nice waves through the window and blocks out his mother's voice. He imagines surfing a tornado, on an ocean, in the middle of all those landlocked places. An ocean smack in the middle of Kansas or Ohio. He thinks about the half joint upstairs in the left pocket of his orange lifeguard windbreaker, and how he will tell his friends about the DWI and how he can joke about it then.

His mother burns the meat loaf, does not curse (she never curses), sort of whimpers to get Timmy's attention. He knows she's still thinking about all that old shit. Once she gets started it can last two days, sometimes more. Maybe it hurts her that he cannot remember, maybe she's just hurt and not angry, because her head, bent over the burnt meat loaf, reminds him of that girl on the beach today who came up to him and thanked him for the great time last night. His mother's eyes go blank in the same way that the girl's did after Timmy asked her name, explained how drunk he'd been, "swilled a pint of Jack." Explained that he did not recall a thing, up until the Coast Guard station, where he puked. The girl, whose name Timmy still did not know, just looked down at the sand, rearranged it a little with her foot, and walked off.

As much as he would have liked to tell his mother and the girl on the beach that yes, he remembered, wasn't it something, he couldn't. He didn't know how. Chowder could have done it easily. Timmy was not clever enough. He had been only three months old when his ears bled, three months old when they moved.

They moved because after Timmy's father got his hand

caught in the lawn mower, he fell in love with the woman doctor who helped rehabilitate the four reattached fingers. He bought a ranch a half-mile from the hospital, even though, Timmy's mother said, "he never rode a horse in his life." Being a devout Catholic, she would not agree to a divorce and moved instead to Rockaway, where her sister was a nun at St. Francis on the Beach, 129th Street.

Timmy spent eight years at St. Francis parochial school, and then close to every night of the next four years drinking tins of Bud on the steps out front. Sister Agnes, his aunt, was referred to as Hagness by everyone, including Timmy, who did not want to be uncool and who saw her beat not a few of his friends. All through grammar school he marveled at the fact that she did not once touch him; she left him to the other nuns or complained to his mother or waited for the rare occasion when she would baby-sit.

His tiny mother is now shaking and twisting her wedding ring. Circles that leave red dents in her skin. She walks to the window that looks out on the ocean and a slight rain, but she seems to notice neither. Timmy gets the impression that she can look right through all the wet and see Ohio, which in his imagination is always yellow and dry. And maybe he's right, because in a moment she jerks her whole body around and looks at the floor, then the table, then the stove like she can't bear looking out there or at anything for very long.

He wonders if she wishes he were young enough to hit. Nuns always have a fresh supply of kids to whack around, but parents have to get it all out before their own kids get too big. Except, of course, someone like Chowder's mom, who has seven or eight kids. That can last quite a while. He wonders if nuns have to confess whenever they beat a kid up or if somewhere Jesus said it was all right since they are nuns. And he wonders if nuns can do regular things like surf and go to the movies and, if so, why they never seem to.

He should know. His own aunt is one; and his mother? Something. Maybe a saint. Really she only hit him once. In the car that time after he ran away from her in Macy's while she was trying on one of those little flowered dresses she wears. And that time hardly counted because it didn't hurt. Even then she had seemed miniature. Timmy, even as a child, felt considerably larger.

He turns off the TV and approaches the spot where she's standing now, quietly. Is she just taking a rest or is she really through bitching at him? Possibly she's praying, which she does a lot, under her breath, barely audible.

"Want me to throw the meat loaf out?"

She doesn't answer, straightens a stack of magazines, pushes appliances back into corners, examines the junk mail she would ordinarily throw out.

Timmy doesn't know what else to do. He begins to search all the cabinets, then inside the refrigerator, where he finds three leftover fish sticks, Wonder bread, dietetic iced tea, and a carton of eggs. He thinks of Chowder's house, where the refrigerator is always packed. He's hungry from having smoked pot all afternoon in the shack and on the tower. It was a boring day, sitting in the rain with nothing to look at but the blurry ocean and no one, no partner, to talk to. Once in a while the black dot of a surfer. Once in a while a stray dog. And then the girl. He should have lied, then maybe she would have stayed.

Some of the other guys spent the day in the shack, partying. They left dummy guards (orange raincoats stuffed with shirts, basketball heads) on their chairs. Timmy couldn't risk getting caught doing anything. He sat lookout, waiting all day to stand up and tap his hat—the universal lifeguard signal for "inspector's coming," meaning time to come back or put out that joint, quick.

He gets an urge to leave the refrigerator door open because it bugs him that there is nothing to eat and because it's the most defiant thing he can think to do. Almost funny how sinful a little thing like that can seem.

"What are we gonna eat?" he finally asks his mother. She is standing very near him. Her eyes, still not meeting his, are wide and black and seem to keep going way, way back someplace watery-dark and real. They remind him of Chowder's eyes that time the two of them took mescaline and sat on the boardwalk scaring themselves into thinking that the gang of Puerto Rican twelve-year-olds on the next bench was going to kill them.

He can tell from her eyes that she's about to start up again. "Twisters, Timothy—you have no idea what it is to look straight in a twister's eye. It can pick up a station wagon, cows, a whole shopping center even."

Maybe she'll cry. In a way he wishes she would. When she cries she looks like some lost kid on the beach who's trying real hard not to cry but can't help it. And that he can handle, can love. It's when she yells that he gets confused, because she looks different and her voice always sounds as if it's trying to go louder than it goes.

But she isn't crying or yelling now, she's just standing there staring, and Timmy gets uncomfortable like he does when girls start to get that way, looking into your eyes all serious and mushy all of a sudden. He hugs her, says, "What are we gonna eat, Ma?" and she hangs on, swaying a little, hurting his neck and laughing quietly, "Timothy," and swaying, "Timothy," very softly like the last clip of one of those sappy old movies she's always watching on TV.

"Want me to get some Chinese or somethin?"

"Not for me."

"Ya sure?"

"I ate a lot of chop meat making the meat loaf."

"Ma, you still mad?"

She lets go of him, straightens her dress even though the kind of dresses she wears, those flowered jobs, never need any straightening or ironing.

"Dogs are mad, Timothy. People are crazy."

Then she turns the TV on and off before any picture has a chance to form, and stands touching the phone with two fingers and not picking it up.

"Maybe I should call Agnes," she says. "She hasn't been feeling well."

Timmy imagines his mother dialing God to ask whether her son has any chance whatsoever. He knows she worries a lot that he does not go to confession. "Do nuns, like, can nuns swim and everything?"

"Why?"

"I don't know."

"Your aunt's a nun."

"So."

His mother looks flustered. Her gray yellow hair sticks out in weird places. Timmy thinks of her alone in the kitchen eating raw chop meat and worrying about the DWI thing and still, after twenty years, feeling out of place around all this water in Rockaway. The thought of the raw chop meat makes him less hungry.

"It's funny," she says, very seriously, "my own sister's a nun and I don't even know." His mother never goes to the beach herself.

"But what do ya think? Maybe they have special suits and everything."

"Well, I don't see why not."

"And if they can swim, they can bowl and eat at Mc-Donald's and everything."

"That's true, they *can* eat at McDonald's, anywhere. Agnes and I have eaten at McDonald's plenty."

This makes Timmy laugh. Maybe his mother and Agnes also get together to eat raw chop meat. Maybe she has forgiven him and everything will get back to normal.

He takes the leftover fish sticks from the refrigerator and eats two of them cold. He tells her not to worry, that he'll pay the fine, that the Coast Guard never shows up like that in the middle of the night, that it was just a fluke, that he did it because he had to get a girl home who was feeling sick and puking and who lived in Broad Channel, across the bay.

His mother tucks loose pieces of her hair back in place. "I'm tired of hearing your cock-and-bull excuses. What's wrong with you, I want to know. Look at Gary next door, he's in Brooklyn College. You just sit on the beach all day smoking marijuana cigarettes and getting picked up in a boat by the—"

"I save people's lives, Ma. What's wrong with that?" But he feels guilty saying this, because it's nearly Labor Day and so far this summer he has saved only one person, a freaked-out old Puerto Rican woman who was in such shallow water her feet could touch bottom. So pathetic a save it was embarrassing. Still, the words "I save lives" seem to work pretty well.

"What about Alex?" she asks. "Don't you see Alex anymore?"

He's never told his mother that he and Alex—his only *real* girlfriend—broke up last spring. "You know she's at school."

"Exactly."

Cruel. Below the belt. He has to try so hard not to think about Alex, while other things it seems so easy not to think about—to forget where he put his car keys, to space out when his mother's talking or when some girl is talking, or

even up on his lifeguard chair if it's too hot or if he drinks
too much Olde English 400 on his break. He lost his virginity to Alex, if it can be said that boys are ever virgins in the
first place, which Chowder does not believe. And he knows
his mother knows that if there's anyone who could make
him do anything, even go to college, it's Alex.

"Why'd ya say that?"

"Because I like Alex."

"That's history, Ma. Alex is old news."

She left for school five very long days ago.

"Well, you can't expect her to hold on to a high-school
dropout, can you?"

He wants to hit her or throw something, but he knows
that'll only make things worse.

"I took the equivalency."

"For what? What are you gonna do with it?"

"I told ya a hundred times, I'm gonna take the fireman
test in September."

"Winter lifeguard?"

Timmy's dying to ask what she ever does besides sort food
coupons, watch detective shows, and reread old issues of
Daily Word, but he's afraid.

"Firemen save people's lives," he says instead and feels
stupid. It's a stupid thing to say.

"What about me and Agnes? It's embarrassing, Timothy.
Look at Gary next door."

"I don't wanna look at Gary, he's ugly, and I don't wanna
go to college, we can't even afford it, and I'm gonna be a
fireman, OK!"

"Look at Alex then."

And that's it. He slams his fist down on the remaining fish
stick and walks out.

"Where do you think you're going?"

"Out."

"You're not even going to shower?"

"No."

"Not a foot in this door drunk tonight, Timothy. You hear? Not a—"

But Timmy can't hear anymore, because he's out the side door. It's still raining a little, and he considers going back for the orange windbreaker with the half joint, but he doesn't know what his mother'll do. Grab onto his shirt or something. Make him sit and play crazy eights around the Formica table or listen to her and Aunt Hagness compete on who knows more Bible passages by heart.

He runs down to the beach to check the waves. The water, a dull green, maybe from sludge or maybe from the sky, is getting darker. The sand blows around in cones that seem to him what tornadoes must be like, only tornado cones would be giant. He stands there, not caring about the sand blowing into his sneakers and his eyes and trying to visualize what Ohio might be like and thinking about Alex. Yeah, she's smart, but also stupid in a lot of ways his mother doesn't know about. Sleeping with Artie and Lefty and lots of guys and not caring who knew because she was going away on scholarship, all summer just killing time till she went away. And maybe his mother is right, maybe she does think he's dumb, because she broke up with him as soon as she got accepted to college.

He's getting wet and bummed out and sick of the beach and sick of the thought of Alex screwing all his friends. It confuses him to hear them talk about her the way they do now, because he doesn't recognize their Alex and he wonders if he's remembering her right.

As he turns to walk back, he sees his mother at the window with his windbreaker around her shoulders the way old ladies wear sweaters, not putting their arms through. She doesn't see him or else sees him and makes no gesture, and it crosses his mind that after he left she ran upstairs for the jacket to give him, which makes him feel bad. The alternative, that she just wanted to wear it herself, makes him feel no better. He walks to the driveway and gets in the car, flicking pieces of fish stick off his hand. He drinks two Schlitzes from the glove compartment and hopes his mother won't or didn't already find the joint in the left pocket, and then he starts up the car.

Driving downtown, he switches on the radio and speeds. He likes those overplayed summer songs because he knows all the words by heart and because they can remind you of particular summers when you hear them three years later in December or February. Singing loudly to "I Want a New Drug," he feels OK again and as if he could just keep on driving, get on some freeway and keep driving to anywhere, Florida or Utah or Ohio. But he has no idea which direction anyplace really is, except New Jersey, where he sometimes goes surfing on his days off. So he pulls up in front of Tubridy's, wolfs down two slices of pizza at Slice of Life next door, and thinks about how he will tell his friends the DWI story. And all of a sudden he feels sort of proud, like some kind of survivor.

When he walks into Tubridy's his friends are in the corner where they always are and already drunk. He's especially glad to see Seaver in his wheelchair among them, and from the look on Chowder's very flat face, Timmy knows they all know what he's planning to tell them. Artie has some girl on his lap whom Timmy does not recognize, but her hair, seriously blow-dried, makes him think she must be from Queens or somewhere out on the Island. She's pretty cute but not gorgeous or anything, a little pimply. He gets a beer and a shot (to catch up) and then walks over. They all hoot, clap, cheer, and this makes Timmy happy. Even the girl looks at Timmy like she's been waiting for him, biding time on Artie's lap.

He tells the story carefully and he exaggerates. Really he does not remember what happened at all. He also tells about the girl on the beach, what big tits she had and what a good time she said she'd had being stopped by the Coast Guard. The girl on Artie's lap makes a face he ignores.

"It was her dad's boat."

Bean wants to know who she was and when he found her—was it when they left him at The Wharf to get clams, because they didn't see him after that?—but Timmy can't say. As the girl on Artie's lap shifts her weight, pink flakes of dried-up calamine lotion fly off her arm. Artie, with streaks of zinc oxide still on his face, smiles lewdly, rubs her leg, says, "Since when does the Coast Guard give a shit? My brother's in the Coast Guard and he doesn't give a shit."

"They're all caring. They're all caring 'cause every Jersey-ite out on his pleasure boat is stewed," Chowder says, bending down to pick off the floor a quarter he's been eyeing. His skin is so sun-battered it looks inside out.

The girl stands up and announces that she's going to the bathroom. They all watch her make her way across the room.

"Where'd ya find her?" Timmy asks, not caring if she hears.

"On the beach. If they look OK on the beach all wet and shit with their makeup all over the place, you know they'll look great later on all fixed up."

Bean picks up her white vinyl clutch bag. "She's not on the rag now," he says, "or she woulda taken this. And she doesn't smoke either, so we all know what's in here, don't we." He picks at his ear, which he does a lot, and everyone laughs, even Timmy, though he doesn't get it.

"So, Artie boy," Bean continues, "you got it in the bag."

Artie grabs the purse and opens it. Takes out a comb, lipstick, wallet, two pens, perfume, and a diaphragm, at which point Timmy understands. He stares at the pile of girls' things, so incredibly alien except the pens, which seem out of place. He wonders if it's all just a cover for the diaphragm and he hopes not. Aunt Agnes never carries a purse, keeps her keys in the long pockets of her robe. His mother has a bag that makes her shoulder hurt. Alex never carries anything.

"She'll be pissed if she sees that," Chowder says, pointing to the stuff on the table. It surprises Timmy that Artie begins putting everything back.

"She be pissing now," Bean says.

"Takes 'em a year in there anyhow, whatever the hell they do in there."

Chowder notices that Seaver has passed out, and he watches to make sure the cripple won't fall out of his wheelchair. Seaver's leaning dangerously far forward, sleeves in a puddle of beer.

"Maybe we should split," suggests Lefty. "Poke a hole in that flying saucer and leave."

But Artie says no, he wants to fuck her. And Chowder says no, it's too unoriginal and "Why don't we find your friend with the boat or rip off some Scotch from my father." And Timmy, as usual, says nothing, thinks nothing. He'll do whatever. Raising his glass to his mouth, he smells fish sticks and pizza and his own sweat.

"One tornado," he starts, "can take your dog into another state, can swallow this whole place up and keep going." His voice is cold, each word hard and separate, like he's speaking a foreign language. His friends, forgetting about the girl, lean forward to listen.

"Tell us about the blood part," Chowder says.

2 | AUTHORITY

He's fed up.

Her legs swing complete afternoons away.

"No," she says, "not a habit. Maybe too much caffeine working in reverse," a comment Chowderhead has no idea what to do with.

"Maybe a nervous disorder." He doesn't say it.

Peg's good as lifeguarding partners go, it's just that as the day wears on she seems to make less and less sense. The radio gets louder. By three, four o'clock there's something zombie in her voice and her legs are swinging so hard that he imagines their old monster of a chair is gonna any second flip. The two of them beneath it like mashed shell.

It was different at first. May, June, the rocking soothed him. He liked the clean arc—legs through air—he liked the way the slats would vibrate ever so slightly. He liked her.

Sure, there were the leftover reasons. Real decent arm for a girl, a slug collection, an ability to blow bubbles inside bubbles inside bubbles. But something new too. Not really a reason, more a sense. It was: Who knows what could happen next. It was suspense. She might do just about anything, soon. It was a feeling like . . . danger.

In July, when the heat peaked, the swinging became almost hypnotic, so he'd sometimes forget—to watch the water, to listen for signals, God, even where he was. Already mid-August by the time he got tired enough of the legs to stop watching altogether. Began, instead, to memorize presidents off a diner place mat. And now September. Those legs, too long, continually cut up, are, he thinks, just begging to be tied down. Just plain fucking annoying.

He turns off the radio and stares at her until she notices. Always a couple of extra swings after the music's stopped, as if someone has wound her up and it's beyond her control.

"Sorry," she says. "You know I forget," she says and pulls her knees up to her chest.

"Yeah, well, all day I've felt like I forgot something," he tells her, but it's more like there's something he's missed.

Peg asks for her windbreaker, which means he has to get down off the chair and go through her bag. He suggests she do it herself, an activity to occupy the legs, but he jumps when her answer's a whine. "I did it last time." Last time? He can't remember and doesn't care. For a moment he considers a swim (not allowed), then thinks about the poker game all set for tonight in his basement.

They can be as noisy as they want because his father, as usual, is away on business. Tulsa, Des Moines, Wichita, one of a list of places whose names Chowder has heard all his life but doesn't know a thing about, except: no water. Enough to dismiss them completely as anywhere he'd ever want to be.

In Peg's bag he finds sunglasses, *his* towel, a petrified-looking ChapStick, and a *Surfer* magazine.

"Not here," he calls up.

"Whataya mean not there?"

"Do you speak English?"

"Shit, then gimme the towel."

He takes his time, does not appreciate being ordered around. Fifty sit-ups with his legs hooked over the bottom rung of the chair—shake *her* up for once. Then he scans the beach for maybe someone to talk to, maybe someone to blow his whistle at.

But action's at a low, weekday and getting cool. One ancient man with his legs crossed, arguing with himself in Spanish. Further down, housewives playing magnetic Scrabble and arguing with each other. Is it a word or isn't it? Their kids eat sandwiches that crunch from sand, or sit in tar, or bury each other up to the neck. Only three fishing boats keep the smooth, shiny Atlantic from total emptiness. A person couldn't feel more useless than this, all day staring at nothing. The diehards who still swam would be in in October, November anyhow. Didn't need *him*. Decked out—full wet suit and booties—January, February.

Chowder takes the towel, his own windbreaker, and the *Surfer* magazine back up to the chair. Peg points to a woman on the shore in what looks like a nightgown, walking a gorgeous, obedient husky.

"She thinks she's floating."

"Don't point." He throws the towel at Peg, as hard as he can get away with.

"The flowing look," Peg goes on, really getting a kick, "dreams of beach sex, foreign countries, and huge, white—"

"Please shut up," Chowder says.

Peg sticks her tongue out, then tries wrapping the towel around herself. But it's from some motel, his father must have brought it back from one of his trips, and it's too small for wrapping, so she just sits and sulks.

"Do you have a hangover? Or do I? You like her, don't you? No, it's the dog, that's more your style. Maybe *you* should get a dog. I mean, maybe if you got—"

"PLEASE?!" Chowder snaps loud enough for the Scrabble crew to stop and turn.

Peg jumps onto the sand, towel flying behind her, then lays herself down right where she lands. He knows he should feel bad but he doesn't. In less than five minutes she's asleep and he can leaf through *Surfer* magazine in peace. Coast of Spain, Hawaii, now we're talking *real* places, water the color of—

"Hey, mister. Yo, mister."

Right next to him, leaning over the chair arm, is this kid, black puffy hair and an incredibly serious expression. Pay attention, the face says, or Don't think you can mess with me, something like that. Chowder's only marveling at how light the kid must be to make it all the way up the tower without budging it, not the littlest creak.

"What's up?" he says to the kid, who's now obviously checking out the view. Hand up to block the sun from his eyes. Eyes the color of water in Hawaii and *that* clear.

"Where be that fat boy at?" the kid asks after a while and real demanding-like, not even looking at Chowder.

"Who?"

"That boy in charge."

He must mean Fleming, the lieutenant, but it's funny, a boy calling a man a boy, and how does he know Fleming and how did he get here without Chowder once spotting him, and, between Fleming and Peg and now this guy, would he ever get just a minute of quiet?

"Well, come on in, I guess," he says and moves over on the bench. "Have a seat."

The kid seems to think about it first, then climbs on but refuses to sit down. Chowder's afraid he'll fall because he's not holding on to anything. He grabs an ankle, size of an adult's wrist, the color of coffee-regular.

"Get offa me," the kid says.

He's got on the cutest blue plastic sandals you've ever seen.

"Whatsamatter," asks Chowder, admiring again, the eyes, girl pretty.

"I'm lost from my muther," the kid says, looking so unfazed it's impossible to know how to react. Can't say "Don't worry"; he doesn't seem worried at all. Can't mush up with sympathy; he wouldn't buy it. This kid is tough.

"What's your name?" Chowder tries instead and puts out his hand for a shake or a slap-me-five.

"What's *your* name?" he wants to know first.

"Chowder," says Chowder.

"That's food," says the kid. "What's your name?"

"I told ya, *Chowder*, now what's yours?"

"Cream-a-mushroom."

Chowder wants to wake Peg up, show this midget off.

"My muther's Angelique," he adds and spits down onto the sand. To watch it fall, probably. The kid sits down on top of his hands, which makes Chowder a whole lot more comfortable.

"And how old are you?"

"Nine."

"Aren't you small for nine?"

"Who says?" straightening up, trying to look bigger.

"C'mon, I gotta know your name."

"Who says?"

"*I* say," says Chowder, sounding ridiculous even to himself, realizing there must be a better strategy. What would Timmy do? Lay on the charm, definitely, give him a Frisbee or something. Peg? Who knows, she probably wouldn't really care what his name was. Sloane, Bean, Lefty, they'd just beat it out of him.

The kid holds the *Surfer* magazine up close to his face as

if his eyes are bad. No way can *those* eyes be bad, but Chowder offers to read to him anyway.

"I can read."

"I know that. I just thought you might like it."

He shrugs and hands the magazine over to Chowder, who shows him the picture of world champion Mark Richards, crouched tiny in a mass of spray.

"This guy," he says, "gets paid just for having fun, playing in the water, and getting a tan."

"So do you," says the kid, but he looks interested, so Chowder reads the quote from Mark Richards in the caption.

" 'I call this the foam rebound.' "

"Like beds?" says the kid.

Chowder nods and continues, " 'The buzz here is in the speed and finding a soft spot to bounce off of. We all need forgiveness.' "

"What?"

"Never mind. He's just getting fancy."

For some reason the kid starts digging one of his nails into Mark Richards. Digs right through the paper.

"What's wrong? Don't you like him?"

The kid shakes his head. No. "I like bikes," he says.

"Bikes? Normal bikes or like motorcycles, dirt bikes?"

"Bikes."

"You got one?"

Again the kid shakes his head.

This is going nowhere. Chowder rolls his windbreaker into a ball and drops it down on Peg. Girls *must* know about these things.

"Leave her alone," the kid says. "She be tired."

"I'm tired and I ain't sleepin."

"So."

"So what if someone was in trouble, what if someone was drownin?"

"You could git 'em."

"Not if I was sleepin."

"You're not."

"If I was."

"Their muther could git 'em."

"What if they didn't have one, or if she was sleeping, or what if they *wandered* away from their mother and started to drown."

"Whoa," the kid says, "low blow." He takes the magazine, throws it down at Peg.

Chowderhead is thoroughly amused. This is not your average lost kid. This is a person. He takes off his whistle and drapes it around the boy's tiny neck. "Blow hard," he says, "just once, nice and short." And they watch as Peg jumps up, charges for the water, then stops, turns very slowly to give him the finger. It really cheers the little guy up and they slap each other's backs, bang on the chair arms and laugh. The kid wants to know if Peg's name's soup too and if she's Chowder's girlfriend.

"No . . . she used to sort of be."

"My girlfriend's Phyllis."

"Phyllis!" Chowder says. "That's a good name. Is she pretty?"

"No." The kid's eyes are on Peg—stomping back, kicking the chair so it trembles, picking her magazine off the sand, and rifling through her bag.

Chowder gets what he's sure is a brilliant idea. "Does Phyllis like your name?"

"No."

Peg announces that Chowder's brain is fried. It's six-thirty and they've been here a half-hour extra for nothing and why didn't he wake her and why are there holes poked in *her* magazine, *her* property.

"Take it easy," says Chowder. "Meet my friend."

"Oh . . . I thought you were talking to yourself. . . . Hi. You guys plan on sittin up there all night or what?"

They climb down. Chowder notices the old man is still arguing with himself in Spanish even though he is asleep. The kid asks again about Fleming in a tone of voice that gives the impression it's his mother who's lost, not him. He's just going about locating her in a calm, reasonable fashion. But there's energy, too. On the way up to the shack he runs ahead and does some impressive flips and cartwheels, then stands, roaring at a mutt eating garbage.

Peg asks, "Is he black or white or what?" and it takes Chowder a second to realize that she means the kid, not the dog. A big knot of hair is sticking up from the top of her head.

"What's the difference? White, I think, just tan, or maybe both. He won't tell me his name."

"Then give him a new one."

Typical Peg approach, but what the hell.

"Mr T!" he shouts, catching up with the kid, scooping him up. "Mr T!" twirling him so fast that the dog gets scared, runs off. The kid demands to be put down but likes it really. His new name as well as the ride. By the time they get up to the shack, he's smiling and giving Chowder the cute plastic sandals to hold. On one of his heels is a miniature blister.

Chowder goes into the trailer that they call a shack and gets a Band-Aid. He's glad to see the place is deserted, positive that Fleming would insist he go down to the precinct immediately, when, well, he was just getting to like the brat. For the first time the concept—kid, one of his own maybe—had become interesting.

Peg says they should at least wait at the shack awhile, a mother might show. They sit outside and carve their initials into the boardwalk with Chowder's keys, the kid saying right off that they aren't his *real* initials because *they*'d be a clue to his name. It's a game that Chowder doesn't mind.

A quiz of presidents' names begins and ends quickly when it's discovered that the kid knows nothing, not George Washington for chrissakes, unless he's lying.

Next, they share a beer that Chowder has stashed in his locker and they rate the girls walking past on the beach. This nine-year-old would have you think he's seen it all already, all sorts of funny things to say—"Too rich," "Sea hag," "Miss Queens." Soon he's riding around in circles on Chowder's bike, until finally they just ride home together, with the kid on the handlebars and Chowder making like he's about to smash into every telephone pole and hydrant on the way.

Maybe he should have stayed longer and waited, but the kid doesn't seem all that concerned anymore, and Peg stuck around only long enough to tell him what to do. His own mother would have given up by now. By now she'd probably be assuming that he was out drinking or surfing or rounding up more guys for poker.

Does the kid know how to play poker?

"Sure."

Chowder is sure he doesn't. Does the kid want to learn?

"Sure."

Chowder is sure he does.

His mother's out back, weeding. Her face is freckly red. It's such a futile effort, growing anything but tomatoes in soil full of sand, he can't understand why she bothers.

"Well, well. Decided to return to the fold, didya?" she says, wiping dirt off her skinny legs. And "Oh!" practically jumping up and down when she sees the kid. "What have we here?," sighing, seeming almost shy, "What eyes!"

He could have predicted it. Seven children before him have grown and gone, and sometimes he thinks that even if he had somewhere to go himself, even if suddenly he had money enough to go to every place he read about in *Surfer* magazine, he wouldn't or couldn't do it.

His mother skips over, stringy ponytail bouncing, and kneels in front of the kid.

"Mr. T," says Chowder. "Meet my mom."

"Hi." The kid also kneels. This makes Chowder and his mother laugh and look at each other.

"Nice house," the kid also says. Even funnier. It's the shabbiest place on the block. Chipped paint, missing shingles, and a basement window that's been broken—was it a year? A souvenir of one of many drunken, midnight football games, and Chowder just hasn't gotten around to replacing it. Makes him curious—where does this kid live, anyway? But he's not about to go fucking things up by asking.

And then the last thing Chowder had expected: a hearty "Hey there!" from the house, from his father, all wet, leaning out a window. The thick white hair on his head, face, chest, really dripping. The thick upper body filling out that small space and looking as if it might get stuck there. Winnie the Pooh style.

"Hi." Chowder smiles, but his greeting is only half sincere. With his father here, poker plans are wrecked. "Scared me." Definitely the old man's intention.

His father has this way of creeping up. Finds it very funny. You're sitting real quiet in your room, say, and he'll tiptoe in, touch your shoulder. No better prey than Chowder's mother, who jumps, yelps, is severely startled every time. But Chowderhead's been conditioned to expect it.

Once, when he begged to stay up late to watch *Dracula*, his father finally gave in, on the condition that when the show ended Chowder would fetch him a wrench from the toolshed. When he later went out in the dark and struggled open the rotted door, his father was *in there*. His father lunged out. "You want a good scare, boy? Hah. I'll give ya a good scare!"

Now he's hanging out of the house and killing or trying to kill some insect in a clap. The fat on his arms vibrates.

"Who's your little friend?" he says. "Wait, I'll be down in a sec." His round face disappears, moments later reappears in the backyard. Enormous red gym shorts and bedroom slippers. Tits. A man with tits. It never even seemed to embarrass him, while Chowder was forever sick about it. Worried about it. As a kid, actually *prayed in church* to be spared this. Forever checking his own chest. Works out the pecs with weights now. Swears they will never, never, ever soften.

"How's my boy?" his father asks as a rule, but this time he pats the kid's head. Leaves his hand lying there.

"Fine. I'm fine. And you?" Chowder wonders whether his father's aware that he's drying his hair with a bath mat.

"You're crushing my brain," the kid says, and, escaping the giant hand, he crawls underneath a hedge.

"So that's where he came from," Chowder's father says. "Hmmm," and then he laughs deeply as his wife explains. Seems there's been problems. Chowder cannot manage to make friends his own age.

What a strange joke for her to make. Chowder wonders whether or not he should be offended. For a moment, the backyard is so silent you can hear Mrs. O'Feely, next door, hosing down her aluminum siding. But before long, his mother becomes festive again, chatters about a barbecue. Real steaks, popcorn, they can put the speakers out the window and everything. Coke? Or lemonade? And there were so many games and toys she just hadn't had the heart to throw away. Now they'd play. Drag 'em all out on the grass and play. Oh, but if she'd known she could've defrosted. Today is so full of surprises and is it all right with Mr. T's mother if he stays for dinner?

So there is no avoiding it.

"Well, ya see, she isn't exactly available, I mean maybe he could stay even longer. We're like ... we've been ... hanging."

The lame ad lib makes his father's jaw droop and fold into a second chin. The kid coughs, then slowly emerges from the hedge like he's hypnotized. Only Chowder's mother retains her smile, though it's obvious she's trying hard. Her eyes, which always bulge, are now wild with interest.

They all stand there and stare, surprised. Not even Chowder had realized what he wanted until he said it. To keep him?

It's silly but doesn't feel silly. Not with the kid saying he's hungry now, like backing Chowder up. Is he? Tension subsiding. Of course, his mother's racing inside for food. Thank God his father's following.

In the driveway, they shoot hoops. No handicaps, on the kid's insistence; "no soft stuff" either. He demonstrates how high he can jump. As high as Chowder's chest. Oh, but if only he'd say something. "I like you." That'd be best. Anything that implied Chowder wasn't alone would do. Like wondering is some girl indifferent to you or just playing hard to get.

Chowder's father sticks his head out the back screen door. Can he speak with him for a moment please, *in private?* Shit. He passes the ball. What now?

The kid asking "You still get beat?" gives Chowder the creeps.

"This backboard is all that gets beat," he says. "Ya hear?" and he walks off. The way he's feeling—might as well have been called in for bedtime while it's still light out. While the whole world's out.

Evidently the barbecue is canceled. Inside smells of spaghetti sauce. Evidently things have changed drastically. His mother whispers "I'm sorry," then turns to plead with her husband. "Your blood pressure, Sam, don't forget." He's pouring too much salt in a pot of water and tapping his foot.

"Who is he? I demand an explanation! NOW!"

"I don't know."

"You know."

"Lost."

"And."

"That's all I know."

"Have you called the police?"

"No."

"Do you plan to? . . . Well?"

Well, what could he say?

"You just don't understand, Dad, it's like, we're really startin—" He ducks the spoon coming at his head. This sort of stuff is usually reserved for his mother, who calls it "the red-headed-devil temper." Long-standing joke how it hadn't gone away although he'd turned gray years ago.

Chowderhead, a redhead himself, decides *he*'ll never tell *his* kid anything that weird. *He*'ll never tell his kid anything. Suddenly he's so confused that the kitchen looks like someone else's.

"DO YOU EVER THINK?" yells his father at the wall. White wall flecked with the sauce he's stirring recklessly. Since when does *he* cook?

"THIS IS NOT ANOTHER ONE OF YOUR STRAY DOGS OR BUM FRIENDS. THIS IS A CHILD!"

Mother's finished smiling. She's chewing on her cuticles. She's backing up into the living room.

"But you wouldn't believe how grown-up, he's a regular—" Chowder doesn't know how to end *that* sentence.

"I CAN'T BELIEVE THIS. I CANNOT BELIEVE THIS." Getting progressively louder. "ARE YOU CRAZY?" Not sure. "HOW LONG HAVE YOU HAD HIM?" Not waiting for an answer. "YOU

WOULDN'T DARE DO THIS IF YOU THOUGHT I'D BE HOME." Not true. "YOU NEED YOUR HEAD EXAMINED. YA KNOW THAT? YOU NEED HELP." Becoming unbearably loud. Beginning to pace. "AND WHAT ABOUT *his* POOR MOTHER? SHE MUST BE WORRIED SICK!" Chowder knew he'd get to that. Notices that his mother, his one ally, has retreated somewhere upstairs.

His father goes to the phone and dials the police. Chowder is impressed that he isn't out of breath after all that shouting. No, he's just shaking his head. For what seems like five minutes he shakes that huge, gray head, then, slamming down the receiver, starts right up again.

"IT'S BUSY!" Like it's Chowder's fault. "WHAT IF YOUR MOTHER WERE BEING RAPED!" A strange image to evoke as Chowder stamps out the door.

So there his father is, all ready to herd the kid into the station wagon and take him away. Chowderhead's stomach hurts. When—miracle, it's so simple—Dad doesn't have his car keys. A "goddammit!" from the house. Sauce boiling over, it must be. A sign? Grab kid, bike, somehow get the two together. Get the hell outta here.

What am I doing? What am I doing, doing, doing, pumping so hard the pedals go too fast for the feet. Why am I doing this? He'll go nuts. He'll be driving around looking for me, he'll *kill* me, well, GO. Where? Timmy's? No, Bean's? No, Lefty's? No, no. God, parents all over the fucking place. Seaver? How could his father call Seaver his "bum friend," Seaver'd never call cops. Were the cops out looking, it's too light, cops out? Oh, why can't this kid *say* something already.

He ditches the bike in some bush and they make for a backyard, then another, then another, this is getting exciting, kid still holding on to the ball. All this time, holding on, he hadn't even noticed, and finally a safe spot, between two fences. He can stop thinking and breathe.

The kid's just sitting there, perched on the ball, calm as ever. He looks bored almost, amused, sort of, it's hard to tell.

"Well?" says Chowder when he can't stand it anymore.

"You been watchin too much TV," says the kid. "You forgot my sandals."

"I never watch TV." A lie. "But isn't this fun? This is fun, isn't it?"

"Sure," the kid says. Sarcastically? Rocking back and forth on the ball. It's soothing. Rhythmic as Peg's legs used to be. And that's what Chowder needs now, with time to consider. All he's got—a shitty bike and four dollars. What a way to start a family. Peg's right. Maybe he should have gotten a dog instead. And yes, his brain *is* fried.

A thin, high whine through the fence.

"Whatsat?" from the kid and the smell of hot butter, steamers, and—

"Lobsters," Chowder says. "Boiling alive."

He's hungry, and by now he's sure the kid's from Far Rock. One of its dark pockets where, stopped at a red light, your mother rolls up windows, locks all doors. Where, late at night, you can go for the only open liquor stores, really holes-in-the-wall, and fronts—things to score. Many things, but none of them lobsters.

"Lemme see those keys again," kid says. To carve his fake initials in the dirt this time, in the fence.

On the other side, guests are arriving, ice cubes are making that sound—silvery, magnified. A discussion of whether to stay outside or go in. It *is* getting chilly, someone says, it's not summer anymore. My Ruth, she left for college last week. Little Ruthie in college? Already? A vote to "rough it," hostess offering jackets? shawls? and wondering aloud where on earth Bob could be.

The kid's still holding the keys but limply, forgetting all

about them. His eyes are enormous, watching through the fence. White blobby things being passed around on a tray, then the clams, chicken wings, corn. In Chowder's panic he had ridden up, not down, and landed them in the rich part of town, where no hungry person should ever be. He's had it now, the last straw, a stray voice exclaiming, "I put it in the guest room because it *looks* like the guest room."

"Let's get outta here, it's dark enough."

He has to pry the kid off the fence, then very quietly walk the bike out. More trespassing. Past a rabbit in a cage, deluxe swing set, sculpture of something and out into a driveway of wet cement. Naturally the kid just has to put his initials in, but, shit, Chowder's keys are gone. Fried brain. Tells the kid to hold on, he'll be back.

Retracing his steps, he hopes the kid won't split with the bike, sees the rabbit take a shit, in pellets, overhears a woman say, "My maid doesn't even believe in evolution. I can't imagine having a decent conversation with her." And a man, "Isn't this better than having a good time?"

Chowderhead thinks about that. He's not having such a good time anymore, but, as the man said, it's better. He feels like part of something important. He almost feels—

Keys. On the ground between the fences. Retracing his steps, he controls a sudden urge to steal the rabbit. He's sure that rabbit would like to be stolen. To be out of its cage, riding around on a bike. But he's not all that sure the kid would want it.

Chowderhead watches as the kid systematically downs a whole roll of Life Savers. With the four dollars they'd also gotten a slice and a Coke each, but, not wanting to risk eating at the restaurant, they'd ridden off, pizza ending up on the blacktop. At a pay phone Chowder calls Timmy, who isn't home, then Peg, who is. He says to meet them near the shack, under the boardwalk. Forgets to say: food, sweatshirts, deck of cards, thanks.

It's a stupid hideout. The boardwalk makes a wind tunnel. After chewing up every last Life Saver, the kid, again on the basketball, asks for a cigarette. He's beginning to get on Chowder's nerves.

"Feel my calluses," he says and brags: He can step on a nail and not feel it. Though he doesn't know George Washington, he can name every pitcher in the major leagues. He once got to second on Phyllis.

"Big tits?"

But the kid just stares, then gets down off the ball and curls up in Chowder's lap.

He asks again about the lieutenant, Fleming. Angelique must know him. Angelique must be young. Angelique—just the sound of the name puts a picture in Chowder's head. Those pictures in *Surfer* magazine. Polynesian women with no tan lines, no straps, flowers in their ears. But Angelique, she'd be better, smaller, and have the kid's eyes.

"It ain't nice," the kid says. "Runnin from ya muther. She's a nice muther."

"What? You ran away?"

"*You*, stupid."

"I did not."

"Did too."

"Did not."

"It's dark under here," says the kid. "Are there rats?"

"It's cold," says Chowder. "Tell me about Angelique."

"She's a secretary—sec-re-tary."

Hawaii dissolves into a new fantasy: Angelique in the office. But the kid keeps interrupting.

"When's it gonna get to be tomorrow?"

"I don't know."

"You're a jerk."

Does he mean it?

"I could get you a rabbit."

Peg approaches out of the dark. She's wearing some weird coat.

"It's my father's," she says, obviously psyched. "It's a spy coat, get it? I'm a spy," she says, sitting down. "Your mother's been all over town. *Every*one knows. . . . Isn't this fun?"

"It was," says the kid. "Till I got frostbit." He finally said it. It was fun. Even after the fact, it makes Chowder happy.

"Got any food? What time is it? Anything on under that coat?"

Peg pulls out a can of soup.

"Are you a retard? How do you expect us to eat that?"

"I didn't think of that. Sorry."

"This is boring," the kid says. "I'm gone." And he gets up, just gets up and starts walking away.

"Did I say something wrong?" asks Peg. "Shit."

There is nothing to do but follow.

"Where ya gonna go?"

"To the party . . . through the fence."

That's two miles away. He'll never find it.

"What party?" asks Peg. She's getting annoyed. "I missed everything."

"*Then* what? When you get to the party?"

"I'll cry."

Smart. Real smart.

"If you come home with me," Chowder tells him, "I'll give back your sandals."

The driveway is packed with cars.

"This is the party," Peg says, "at your house?" Chowder tells her his parents don't have friends in the police department, but as they walk inside he's not so sure. Kitchen's full of them. Cops, eating spaghetti. And they're all looking pretty chummy. That is, until they see *him*.

"Thank God," sighs Chowder's mother. "Thank God your father's still out looking." But you can barely hear her over Chowder's friends, all there, he realizes, for the poker game. Timmy, Bean, Artie, and Louie the Lump eating spaghetti. They hoot, cheer, whistle like Chowder's a hero.

A pock-faced cop yells "Quiet!" but continues eating after he tells someone to call the precinct. Then he lights a cigarette and asks the kid if he's all right.

"Sure," the kid says. "Can I have some of that spaghetti?" Which provokes the inevitable mothering fit. You poor little thing. You must be famished, and on and on, blah blah.

The cop tells Chowder to "sit down, young man." So he crouches in the only available space. On the floor, next to the kid. He eyes the bowl of spaghetti.

"Son, are you aware that kidnapping is a federal offense?"

"Um."

"Do you have any idea of the seriousness of a federal offense?"

"Um."

"Excuse me," Peg says. "But it's not a federal offense unless he crossed state lines."

"She's right," from another cop. "He's got himself a lawyer." Across the kitchen, uncontrollable nodding. His mother and the poker gang.

"As I was saying, the penalty for kidnapping happens to be life imprisonment." All motion stops. "Do you hear me? *Life.* Now I am sure—"

"How do you know it's kidnapping?" Peg asks. "How do you know the kid didn't wanna go?"

"Look, Miss, I am not interested in your opinions; this matter does not concern—"

"It's not an opinion."

"Feisty," says the nice cop, and the boys all agree. She's something. Especially those legs, huh? They're all experts suddenly. You should see her surf, shotgun beers. All of them talking at once, and what Chowder fears most is not this cop or jail or court but his father, who might appear at any moment. Pockface gives up trying to shut everyone up and just shouts over the general chaos.

"Whether we are discussing kidnapping or child stealing or reckless endangerment is not for us to decide. I was merely trying to point out the gravity of this situation." Then, turning toward Chowder, "Are you ready?"

"Who, me?"

"Who else?"

"But—"

"I'm assuming handcuffs will not be necessary."

"But—"

"LET'S GO!"

Chowder jumps to his feet. His mother's throat makes sounds like a dog caught in barbed wire.

"Can I finish my spaghetti?" the kid asks, innocent as hell. Cop says OK but hurry. Chowder's mother's freckles seem to smear as her face twists. Bean says, "Heavy shit. Does this mean the poker game's off?" And the kid says, "Lucky you didn't steal the rabbit, too."

"What rabbit?" say five or six people.

Chowderhead is scared. He didn't think it'd be this big a deal, and he's never been arrested all by himself before.

"How'd you know all that stuff?" the nice cop is asking Peg.

" 'Perry Mason,' I think."

"Where'd you get those eyes?" he's asking the kid.

"From my head."

The little guy's torturing everyone, eating the spaghetti strand by strand. But he's a novelty.

"He's sharp."

"He's cute."

"He's a regular comedian."

"Nope," the kid says. "He's a runaway."

"WHAT?"

Oh, Chowderhead could kiss him but only winks instead, and the kid goes on, quite an actor. How he got in this *terrible* fight with his mother. How Chowder spent the entire evening trying to convince him to go home.

"Well," says the nice cop. "That changes everything." The boys are giving a round of applause, Peg's nodding, Chowder's mother is in shock.

"Hold on," says Pockface. "How come you waited till now to tell us all this?"

He's just dying to nail someone. He obviously hates Chowder's face.

"My muther says I ain't s'posed to talk with my mouth full," the kid says, grinning.

Chowder doesn't know whether he's an angel or only the coolest human being he's ever met. Phyllis is a lucky girl— and Angelique? He is almost sorry that he won't get to meet her after all.

His mother is apologizing. There is no dessert in the house. But would anyone care for some coffee? No, no thanks, we've really got to get going. Thanks so much, though. We're so glad everything worked out. She sends Timmy out to find her husband.

"Stay outta trouble," says Pockface to the room as he slaps Chowder's back as hard as he can. Then he leaves, all dramatically, the way cops do.

Chowder follows the kid out. "Aren't you gonna say goodbye?"

The kid's inspecting the police car. "Wild." He says to the nice cop, "Can we git the sirens going?"

"But—"

They get in the car. Chowderhead watches. His stomach hurts.

As they pull out, he trips over the basketball, and all at once it seems urgent that he give the ball to the kid. He runs after the police car, but the cop won't stop. One half-wave from the kid out the window and they're gone. He's gone, and Chowder remembers the sandals, still somewhere on the lawn.

In the empty street, Chowder bounces, bounces the ball. So hollow a sound it's like it's from the inside. Every sort of hunger coming together in that familiar thump. Thump. Thump.

And then, out of nowhere, Peg, kissing his neck. A ploy to snatch the ball. She's got the ball. She's laughing, dribbling it away. Effortlessly circling cars, trees, then coming back, under her legs and around Chowderhead. She's good. Maybe he'll show her the swing set.

3 | BEING "IT"

Cicadas are drawn to the green stripes on orange lifeguard bathing suits. Fly directly at you in their fat, blind cicada way, while mosquitoes, they circle with a purpose. Hover, then strike. And biting flies are silver black with green eyes. Once moths become moths they have no stomachs or mouths and they die.

Timmy lists insects to stay awake on the tower. To stop thinking of Alex. To test the brain cells his mother is convinced he's destroying. Hundreds of them at a time.

He read that, about the moths, almost a month ago. That proves his moth brain cell's still intact.

He examines the upside-down cicada on his hip. It must not care about being upside down since its legs aren't moving. It's the eighth one on his hip so far today.

"Number eight," he tells his partner, Sloane, and flicks it off.

"I just leave 'em," Sloane says. "I'm sick of flicking, I just leave 'em."

Timmy checks Sloane's suit for cicadas, expecting a whole row. Four or five maybe. None. One measly fly on the chair arm. He wonders if it's true what Alex once said: "Flies throw up every time they land." But there is no visible vomit. In places where Sloane's hairy arm makes shadows, the wood of the chair looks darker.

"You're it!"

"You're it!"

At first they sound like girl voices, so high and hysterical-like, but, turning to look, Timmy sees about five boys scattering on the dry sand.

"How long have my eyes been closed?"

"Coupla hours," says Sloane, laughing. They watch the game. "What's that called again?" Sloane wants to know, "That game, what's that called?"

"Peas and butter." The peas-and-butter brain cell is fine.

"Yeah, that's it."

"You're it."

A new round. The towel is buried. Home base is a wire trash can.

"Hot peas and butter! Come get your supper!" wails "it," in this case a fairly big kid, pinkish limbs and a thumb up his nose. Then the fun begins: who can find the rat-tail weapon.

Yes, it's the same game Timmy and Sloane once played, except they used belts.

"Warmer, you're getting warmer," and, "Coolish . . . freezing." As soon as the wet towel's found, twisted up, clutched in the fist, it's—POWER. No limit to the whippings.

"Those were the days, huh?" Sloane says. "Now ya gotta take it out on your girlfriend."

Timmy doesn't answer. He thinks of the time he came home with a bruised face from some kid's, possibly Sloane's, unfair belt buckle, and how his mother made him pray. She made sure.

Yeah, those were the days. He leaves Sloane to watch the game, turns back around. Checks the water and resumes his list. Tells himself he's safe on his chair, the high chair. Old and safe. But the sounds keep coming at him and he is not that old.

Spiders and walking-sticks and those little white bugs that invade plants and boxes of cereal. There are more species of bugs than of all the other animals put together. There are more bugs in one acre of a field than there are people in the entire world. The tide is getting high.

"Know anything about bugs?" he asks.

"Yeah," Sloane says. "They're real easy to kill."

Timmy licks the sweat off his upper lip and rubs his eyes. Alex said she once fell asleep driving. Woke up five miles later, not swerving or anything.

He tries to picture this and then Alex at college. Her thick, funny hair when she sleeps on it wet. Wood-color hair to match the summer skin, and eyes bluer and lighter than smoke. She's casually rushing, she does that. Only now it's with books toward cafeterias. Or with strangers into libraries. It bothers him that his brain cells cannot do any better. Termites and praying mantises.

He takes out his empty, tuna-smelling lunch bag and starts a letter.

Dear Alex,
How are you? I'm fine except for falling asleep. Also my nose is peeling off. Did you know that girl praying mantises bite off their boyfriends' heads right after they screw? It's true. I read it in *National Geographic*.

No. She would think that was stupid. He crosses it out, then lifts his leg to block the letter from Sloane.

Sloane has big legs that take up three-quarters of the seat. He has recently recovered from the hepatitis he got swimming around Manhattan Island on a dare. Water so brown and smelling so bad you wouldn't even bother saving yourself from drowning in it.

"Got any J's?" Sloane asks, smoking an invisible joint.

"No, you?"

"No."

Ants, spiders, lightning bugs. She wouldn't be interested. He crumples the bag up and plays catch with himself. Throwing it up with one hand, catching it with the other. The tide is getting high.

Beach packed with greasy flesh, damp hair, garbage. Kids splash or ruin each other's castles or beat each other with towels. Old ladies read paperback mysteries under umbrellas, their suits with skirts attached. Teenagers play Frisbee or make out by the wall. Cigarettes and ankle chains.

"Ice-cold soda!" sings the vendor in long pants. "Diet for the fat ladeeees, regular for the skinny ladeeees. Ice-cold soda!" Timmy can never understand how the soda stays even remotely cold in a brown shopping bag.

"You gonna help me with the horns this time," asks Sloane, "or you gonna be a wimp again?"

"Depends on the chore."

First-year lifeguards go through a sort of initiation hazing that Sloane loves to administer.

"Got any ideas?" he asks in a way that implies "I do."

"Well, we could buy some hamburgers and all spit on 'em and give 'em to Shaughnessy or that guy with the teeth missing."

"Rogers?"

"Yeah."

"I don't know. See, I was thinkin of somethin a little more, ya know."

"Sick?"

"Interestin's a better word."

"Sick is what you mean."

"You're gonna wimp out again, I can tell."

Timmy closes his eyes, just for a second, sees purple and tiny sparkling white things. When he was a horn he got tied to a pole naked and beat with a toilet brush dipped in green paint. A fate you could say was lucky. Some guards are eternal horns—eternally horned. One guy quit when they told him to stand with his foot in a bucket of water and his hand on a pole during a thunderstorm.

"You chickenshit maggot."

"I said I'd help," Timmy says. "Dependin on what it entails."

"Big fuckin word, 'entails.' How come you didn't go to college usin big fuckin words like that."

They watch a girl in a yellow bikini pointing her foot at the water.

"Hey you in the blond!" Sloane yells at her.

She moves closer and puts on the sunglasses she is carrying. Covers up the dents Timmy has noticed on the sides of her nose.

"Whoever said girls with glasses never get passes?" Sloane says, leaning forward.

"Dorothy Parker," the girl says, smiling, walking away.

Timmy laughs. "Blew it, stud."

Sloane waves his elbow, says, "She's a fuckin dog anyway," and, "Who the hell is Dorothy Parker?"

"I don't know."

"I think she's got a talk show or somethin. Ain't she that mornin talk show woman with the giant hair?"

"I don't think so," Timmy says, putting zinc oxide on his nose. Alex would know, she went to college. Probably the girl in the yellow bikini went to college.

"So, you gonna ask what I have in mind for the horns or what?" Sloane asks.

"You're gonna tell me whether I ask or not."

"You're a fuckin drag, ya know that?"

"Yeah," Timmy says, flicking the ninth cicada off his hip.

"I wish you were a horn, I'd have somethin real nice planned out for you." He blows his whistle, motioning for a group of swimmers to move left, away from the jetty.

"What'd the guys do to you?" Timmy asks, wondering if Sloane was born cruel or picked it up later, lifeguarding.

"Pissed all over me," Sloane says happily. "Then stuffed me in a locker and left me face down on the boardwalk overnight."

"Why don't you use that one on Rogers?"

"The trick is, see, you gotta be original about it. Ya know, cre-a-tive."

The image of Sloane's big legs stuffed in a little locker is pleasing to Timmy. He goes on with his list out loud.

"Roaches, leeches."

"Leeches aren't bugs," Sloane says. "But they're fun. See, now you're thinkin. They could feast like royalty on Rogers . . . yeah. Where do you get one of those, anyway?"

"You are one of those."

Obviously fed up with him, Sloane puts on his Walkman. He has this theory that you don't need to hear the whistles if you just look around enough.

But sitting with a guy wearing a Walkman is like sitting one-man. Lifeguard punishment for carelessness. DWI in a boat. Messing up the sign-out sheet. Falling asleep.

He will not fall asleep. Ladybugs. Maybe Alex wouldn't think the praying mantis fact was dumb. Maybe she would be impressed. He smooths out the bag and rewrites what is crossed out, then adds:

Came to work really hungover today and did the old oxygen trick. What happens if the pure oxygen runs out when we really need it? Every morning there's a line by the tank. But it's amazing how well it works. Every home should have some.

Last night was Chowderhead's birthday. We went to Beefsteak Charlie's and beat the check out the bathroom window. Then Chowder wanted to go down to Playland and curse out our old boss, and since it was his birthday I had to. But luckily it was closed when we got down there. I know you just left, but when are you coming home next? Do you know who Dorothy Parker is?

He crosses the last line out and changes it to "Wasn't it Dorothy Parker who said, 'Girls with glasses never get passes.' " That will have to impress her, even though she's got perfect vision. Then he writes, "What do you think moths did before the lightbulb was invented? Did you know moths live a week at most? Isn't that sad? Do you have a boyfriend up there? I wish you'd—"

There is no room left on the bag. Rereading, Timmy sees that a lot of what he's written is made invisible by dark spots where mayonnaise has dripped. He puts the bag in his knapsack and writes on the chair arm: "Timmy was here. 9/6/86." Tries to dig it in hard, but the pen tip breaks and splatters ink all over his hand up to his wrist.

Bleeding from Sloane's Walkman is Iron Maiden or Quiet Riot or something equally noisy. Alex used to call Sloane "Noisy," because of the way he screams out his car window or off the tower at girls and leads the chant "Murderer" at all Death Kegs, those famous wake parties after a drowning. Yes, Sloane's big on ritual. If it isn't horning or Death Kegs, it's the five-mile run on dry sand at noon. Washing his car every other Friday. The logistics in creating nightmarish bachelor parties.

"I say we paint Rogers black, tie him to a stretcher, and

set him out to sea," Sloane says very loudly. "Is that great or what?" He takes off his headphones.

"Well?"

"Interesting," Timmy says.

Sloane jumps off the chair, singing, "Maggot, maggot, maggot," and takes a package of Alka-Seltzer out of his pocket: Timmy watches him wrap it in a piece of bread left over from his lunch and feed it to a seagull. Old lifeguard pastime. The bird's insides explode. They make a noise like a faucet being turned on. To watch it happen is always disgusting and fascinating, both. The closest Timmy's come to anything like it himself is knocking a few pigeons out with shells or BB's.

"Wait, wait a second!" Sloane yells, climbing back up. "I got it, I got it!"

"Could you at least chuck that gull somewhere where I don't have to look at it?"

"I'm eating him for snack time." One time Sloane had pointed out to him a whole crew of old women cooking gull under the boardwalk. "Listen," Sloane says, "You gotta hear what I just thought up."

Timmy notices blue ink on his waterproof watch. "Get that thing outta here first."

Sloane ignores him and goes right on talking. "We make like there's someone drownin and Rogers didn't notice. Start divin for this invisible swimmer, see, and really freak him out! Make him think like he let some kid drown."

"You're a genius," Timmy says.

"Ain't I?" Sloane makes a muscle. "Man, I shoulda been a writer or somethin with all these great ideas."

Sloane's last great idea was to go up to a family whose father had just drowned and say, "More room in the car on the way home." "More room in the car!" while they're bawling their heads off.

If Timmy had another bag he'd write to his own father. Brag—he placed first in Lifeguard Olympics two years running for butterfly. Ask—is riding a horse like riding a surfboard? Then inevitably trash the letter like he always does.

Dragonflies, horseflies, mayflies. Mayflies only live one day. Timmy gets down off the chair and finds a piece of newspaper to cover up the dead seagull. Its eyes are open. Then he climbs back up and tries not to think about it. The ink won't come off his watch. Four-fifty, only a little time left.

Fewer swimmers now and the tide getting higher. The bead vendor looks as if he's had a bad day with all his cheap beads still left hanging off his forearm. Soda man's doing better, Timmy can tell, because he's able to walk faster with a lighter bag. Still, he stops every few yards to empty the sand from his cuffs. Boys' game below still goes on full force. "Hot peas and butter! Come get your supper!" and the towel snaps.

Timmy watches Sloane scratch a mosquito bite completely off. Blood swells in a circle.

"Oh my God!" Suddenly Sloane's yelling, running toward the water. "Oh my God!" His hands straight up in the air, the submersion signal. Timmy following: "What? What happened? What?"

"Didn't ya see her go under? Shit, the girl with the glasses, didn't ya see, asshole? Dive over there!"

The swimmers run out of the water or tread in place and Timmy dives, right away realizing he's been had. Sloane's just bored again. Sloane's got nothing better to do than to humiliate him in front of a bunch of ten-year-olds.

Underwater's warm, cushioned, so he figures he'll stay awhile. Since he's already made a complete idiot out of himself, he might as well be one in private. Try to imagine live things—bright twirling insects, gulls, flexing wings, and

Alex, in college, in a yellow bikini. But Alex never wears bikinis, and he has to breathe. He has to come up eventually.

And out there, laughter. Sloane's Fred Flintstone bellow and a chorus (higher pitched) behind. Some delirious old guy yelling "Good one! Good one!" and patting Sloane's pimply back and telling him he used to be a lifeguard too, which Timmy already figured.

In the too-bright sky, flying banners advertise Cruex and Native Tan. On the shore, this ugly frizz-headed kid says, "You looked so funny with your white nose." And Sloane, "Man, that was a cinch. Scared ya good, huh?" Timmy just keeps walking, blushing, toward the chair—the throne. His legs feel boneless.

"Lighten up, dude. I was only tryin to prove a point. It's easy, see. I just want your help. It's easy." And Timmy, too tired to disagree, hurries back up the tower and sees that ink and water together have turned his hand blue. Through the noise in his brain, he can hear Glasses Girl scream "Fuckhead!" at Sloane and the game of peas and butter resume.

"Warm, very warm, hot, hot burning, you're *it*!"

4 | LETTERS

Dear Alex,

How are you? Right now I'm waiting for a phone call from this guy who told me he could get me a job at Fish-R-Us. That's about all. The fireman thing looks pretty bad since the list just to take the test is three blocks long. I guess I could join the Coast Guard or try to be a cop or something but I don't know, I'll see about this Fish-R-Us thing. What are you taking at school? Is it hard? Chowder's brother (in college) told me sometimes he does speed and stays up all night studying. Can you get speed? He says not sleeping makes you feel like you're on drugs. Is that true?

Chowder's brother is going to be a gym teacher. It's weird to all of a sudden have to be something. Will you write back? The phone's ringing.

Love,
Timmy

Timmy — Thanks for your letter. Did you get the job? I always thought it was funny that Fish-R-Us

is right next to Toys-"Я"-Us. School isn't that hard.
Mostly I'm studying anthropology, about Indian
tribes and stuff. It's true about staying up to do
work, but I don't do speed since the time I saw this
girl's nose drip blood down the straw. Not sleeping
is like a drug, also not eating. See you — Alex

Dear Alex,

   Thanks for your postcard. Your handwriting got
tinier than it used to be. How come? It's really tiny.
I hope you're eating. Can't you get speed in pills
instead of snorting? Don't think I'm a druggie.

   I didn't take the job because it turns out to be
less money than I already get at the deli, plus bus
fare out of Rockaway. I can't even get out of here
as far as Bklyn. What's New Hampshire like? Isn't
that where you and Peg used to go to camp and hit
bats with tennis rackets? I always remember that
for some reason. It's pretty dull now that the summer is officially canned. Yesterday a ten year old
beat me in paddleball. He told me I owe him a beer.

   I know that we're supposed to be friends now and
everything but I still think about you a lot. Also my
mother asks why I'm writing to you if you broke up
with me. She's going on this retreat with St. Francis
next weekend if you maybe want to come down and
stay over. Maybe. I hope that doesn't piss you off.
Please write back.

Love,
Timmy

Timmy — My handwriting is tiny so I can fit it all
on a postcard. Also it got smaller, I just feel like

writing that way now. New Hampshire has a lot of trees and farms, also bats. I guess you can find speed in pills but all the bats in N.H. snort. I am eating. Say hello to your mother for me — From Alex   P.S. I went to camp in Pennsylvania. Have you seen Peg?

Dear Alex,

How are you? I had a big party last night since my mother was on that retreat. She's got to fast and everything, maybe she'll have a drug-like experience. My party was all right but there's still a lot to clean up and a chair leg to Crazy Glue. I kept thinking that maybe you'd show up as a surprise even though your card didn't say anything about it. I kept thinking other girls were you. Also I slept on the couch because I lent the bedrooms to Chowder and Bean. The two girls they slept with turned out not to be such hot friends and the morning was kind of tense. Peg's around. She dropped out of Kingsborough and is selling subscriptions to *The Wave*. I don't think I'm going to go out tonight. Rot-a-way, you know. Do you have a roommate? Are the parties at Camden like the ones in *Animal House*? It's nice to have someone to write to.

Love,
Timmy

P.S. I saw some baby rabbits in the empty lots by Playland. Rumor has it, Frank Sinatra owns those lots in case they ever build casinos here. Then, they'd really be worth something. There are also new sorts of gulls with black beaks that can catch crackers in mid-air. OK, bye again.

Timmy — Hi. Thanks for the party update. Won't ol' blue eyes look snazzy playing blackjack in a rabbit fur suit? What girls did Chowder and Bean sleep with this time? Why did Peg drop out of school? Any other new Rockapulco gossip? Yes, I have a roommate. She's from Chicago. She's all right. Her father invented the first ready-made pancake batter. She's pretty rich. The parties here aren't exactly like Animal House since there are no fraternities but they do get out of hand. Mostly they have themes, i.e., Dressed to Get Laid, Black and White, Gidget Goes Hawaiian, Dressed to Repel. See you — Alex

Dear Alex,

School sounds fun, I would like to visit. Do you dress up for those parties? Did you make that all up, the names? Chowder slept with Alicia, you know that prom queen girl who works in Mickey's Deli with us. Bean slept with Carol, I don't think you know her. But now Chowder's seeing Carol and Alicia hates us. She tells the boss every time we come to the store late. She's a real bitch. Is that good gossip?

Mike Sloane's mother died in a car crash on the Cross Bay Bridge. His father was driving drunk and might go to jail. Mike's acting the same even though everyone is being really nice to him. He still says mean things and starts trouble. All these girls were all over him last night and he went home with—guess? Alicia. Maybe she's not a bitch, just weird.

I started thinking about my father again. That reattached finger thing can really give you the creeps. My mother gets all upset when I ask her about him. Says I ruin her peace like she's turned hippie or something. She talks about her peace a lot since she came back from the retreat. Once I got a Christmas card from my father when I was five and she burned it. Did I ever tell you that? I miss you a lot. Do you ever think of me? I feel like I should like Sloane now that his mother died but it's hard, he's so—What do you think? Write.

Love,
Timmy

P.S. Peg got kicked out of school. Something about fire extinguishers.

Dear Timmy, I'm sorry to hear about Sloane's mom but you shouldn't feel bad if you still don't like Mike. Think of when he stole our clothes that night we were swimming. He's an asshole. Even assholes' mothers die. I'm sure your Dad thinks about you, he probably feels guilty. I do know Carol if her last name is Sullivan. She was in Girl Scouts with me and Peg. Fire extinguishers? Carol and Chowder, huh? Interesting. Bye. Alex

Dear Alex,

That skinny-dipping night was my birthday. Remember? I was glad Sloane stole our clothes and you got mad, made me go to my house naked. But you looked so cute in my pants. You had to make six cuffs since they were so long. There's other things I remember too. Do you? Don't you think we had fun?

Carol and Chowder aren't going out anymore. Carol has a new boyfriend from Brooklyn. He's got mega-tattoos, you can see them coming out the top of his shirt all the way up to his neck. Chowder says he didn't really like her all that much anyway, but he keeps talking about starting a fight with the new guy, for kicks.

You didn't answer about visiting. Would your roommate care? Does she eat a lot of pancakes? I'd like to think up some invention. Lately, I wonder what my father does for a living but my mother would have a fit if I brought it up. Maybe he's a fireman. Sloane's dad isn't going to jail but he's going to a detox hospital on Long Island somewhere. Sloane says he wants to have a party with the house to himself, but I don't think I could handle it. This girl said she may be able to get me a job cleaning airplanes at Kennedy Airport. She says you find all kinds of valuable stuff. What are you dressing up as for Halloween? I'm going to be Geraldine Ferraro or a fireman. I miss you, Alex.

Love,
Timmy

Dear Alex,
     Why don't you write me back anymore?

5 | THREE'S A CROWD

Alex's roommate separates her eyelashes with a needle, says, "You should do this. You've got a lot of clumps." Her nose whistles when she breathes in.

Alex watches the tiny flecks of falling blue mascara and hums inside her head and thinks about sleeping or reading Roommate the letter from Timmy. The letter where he says Alex is the smartest person he knows.

Someone kicks at the door. The needle keeps going, sometimes catching the light. Alex blows across an empty Beck's bottle. Two more kicks. Then two more. "What if it's someone good?" she finally says.

"Someone good?"

"What if it's not Lars."

"His name is Larry."

"What if it's not him?"

"If it's not him, what do I wanna answer the door for?"

"You said you were hiding from him."

"I am. How does this eye look?"

"Looks the same," Alex says without really looking.

"It can't." She starts on the other eye. One lash at a time. From base to tip.

Amazing to Alex, who jumps at every kick. "You shouldn't do that drunk," she says, and, after a moment, "I thought you hated him."

Roommate gives a look like "I can't believe how stupid you are," then mouths, "There's no one else to like."

Alex thinks of the possibility that it's Joe—her heart-throb—kicking at the door. More than doubtful. She saw him an hour ago in the all-night study room, speaking bad Spanish to that guy from Brazil.

"Are you going somewhere?" asks Alex.

"No."

"Then why are you doing that to yourself?"

"Just in case."

Roommate sleeps with makeup on just in case Lars should happen to drop by in the middle of the night. And wears her diaphragm everywhere, to class even, just in case.

More kicking. Alex begins humming again, this time out loud. Roommate puts on a sweater, Alex's sweater, then just stands there, smiling at the wall. The kicks get further apart and softer, almost pleading. Different from Lars's usual style. Usually, he's got an alternate female lined up in case Roommate is not in the mood to open the door.

Alex realizes she's been humming Billy Idol, "Flesh for Fantasy," and stops. She tells Roommate she's answering the door. Someone could be out there bleeding to death.

"You are not."

"Cut the shit, you wanna see him."

Roommate looks at herself in the hand mirror, killing time, Alex thinks. Then she says, very slowly, "I'm not finished putting on my makeup."

"I hope you're drunk," Alex says. "Otherwise you've totally lost your mind." Then she goes to the door.

Lars will be out there, sitting on the floor, saxophone strap still on, always on. But no, no one in sight. A few empty beer cartons, one bed frame, and a Snickers wrapper. "Flesh for Fantasy" is playing two doors down and Alex can smell bad pot, damp wool, wonders if it's raining. No Lars around. No Joe.

"Maybe it was the wind," she says, shutting the door. Roommate hands her the swill left in the bottom of her beer. Alex looks down at the small pool of liquid, then gives the bottle back and walks to the window. No rain. At least none she can see.

"I'm supposed to do an oral report tomorrow," says Roommate, cleaning her nails on the edge of an envelope. "I like completely forgot."

The envelope is from Timmy's letter. Alex left it out so Joe might notice. Still, she doesn't like Roommate sitting there, with *her* sweater on, cleaning her nails on Timmy's envelope. Good old Timmy, with his big, silly shoulders from doing the butterfly year after year. Good old Timmy, exhaustingly loyal to everything.

Joe is nothing like him, nothing like any of the guys Alex is used to. It's not a physical thing, although a thin, dark type in Rockaway is rare, and although lifeguards can't wear glasses. What is it, then? Joe talks more, eats less, something. Has good handwriting. The walls of his room covered with photographs he took himself. A whole graveyard series from a place nearby. Tombstones with no names, just "Mother," "Wife," like that. He wears button-down shirts with no one forcing him and he likes to dance. The guys at home would call him queerbait. Alex picks up Roommate's hand mirror, holds it up to her face. Her face looks bigger, while her eyes, a sticky, dull blue, seem to have shrunk.

"Do I really have clumps?" she asks.

Then another knock at the door. Alex walks right over and answers it. It's Ponzio, the chess whiz with spike bracelets and hippie hair, standing there looking away, at something down the hall.

"Some guy on the phone for you."

It's Joe, Alex can tell before he says anything, by his cough. Can he borrow her car? he wants to know. He and the Brazilian are hungry. Alex says OK even though they don't invite her. Joe talks constantly to the Brazilian while he's still on the phone.

She hangs up angry with herself for saying yes like that, right off. With the phone book she kills two flies and then isn't angry anymore but a little sad. Flies die so easy in the fall. All slow and fat.

She returns and finds Roommate polishing her nails. Plum. The color of the bruises you get after you slam your fingers in the door, right before the nail falls off.

"Who was that on the phone?"

"Joe."

"You still on *that* leash?"

Alex decides not to mention that she's offered to lend him her car. He only said he "might" want to borrow it anyway. She doesn't like how good her sweater looks on Roommate.

"Maybe he's on *my* leash?" she says.

"What the hell for? He's a dork. God, Alex, how could you like that guy?"

"How could you like Lars-with-the-twitch."

"Larry does not have a twitch, he has bad circulation."

"Ah, yes, and his hands show evidence of stigmata."

"Is he any good at least?"

"What?"

"In bed, moron, what do you think?"

"Well, I never actually slept with him."

"C'mon, *everyone* knows you're sleeping with him."

How can she argue with that, with Everyone? She wishes she was, says, "I am not."

"Then what do you do all the time? All that time with him, what do you do?"

Alex doesn't know what to say. She's tired. The last thing she did with Joe was go to Price Chopper at four a.m. They walked up and down the aisles eating as much food as possible and then bought a pack of gum. Is that what he planned to do with the Brazilian?

"Maybe I should bleach my moustache?" Roommate says, blowing on her nails, waving her hand around wildly.

Alex begins her essay on Matriarchal Societies with the line "There are many cases of matriarchal societies." Then she puts down the notebook and goes back out the door, toward the bathroom. Two stereos battle it out in the hall. One playing "Girl, I Want Your Body," the other, "I Want Muscle." Passing Ponzio's room, she considers knocking and asking for a bong hit, but she hears some girl either crying or laughing through the door and keeps walking.

She brushes her teeth and pees and covers the blackheads on her nose with Clearasil cover-up stick. The package says, "For Great Looking Skin Even Close-Up." Then she tries unclumping her eyelashes by pulling at them, and ends up with a hair in her eye. She has to go back and ask Roommate for help.

"Incompetent," Roommate says, pulling the top lid over the bottom.

"It's still in there," Alex says, rubbing the eye.

"Don't rub!"

Her eye is all weird and watery now so she can't go on with her essay. Can't do anything but lie on her bed and wait for Joe. Stare at the wall.

Her wall isn't all cluttered like Roommate's. She doesn't even like the one thing hanging, a postcard from her mother. It stares. Originally, she threw it out, but then she got to thinking—what if her mother died or something? Then the card would all of a sudden be significant. All that guilt, she might never recover.

There's another problem with things on the walls. They stop getting looked at. Two days on the wall and you're already sick of your favorite picture. Your favorite picture that you'd still love now if it wasn't hanging on your wall all this time. The way Alex loved Joe because he only said "might come," and loved her mother because she might die.

Roommate tweezes her eyebrows, shaves her legs, applies rouge to her cheeks and announces she's going to sleep. Turns the lights off without waiting for Alex to say anything.

Alex thinks of waiting in the hall for Joe but doesn't want to seem anxious and wonders will he come alone or with the Brazilian and will he invite her?

From the bed she can see out the window. Lighted rooms. Trees. Five different kinds of black. She can hear wind blowing gravel from the paths and her roommate trying to masturbate quietly. She wishes that something would change. That she could change and be—what? That someone would take the eyelash from her eye. That she could go to sleep and not care, that she had written her essay, that she could climb in bed with Roommate without feeling strange. Just to be near someone.

Joe. Hard to follow but easy to meet. On line at food service he turned around, just turned around like he knew her and asked if maybe she'd like to go out to eat. The beef Stroganoff, he said, was gray. She went, mostly for the hell of it, mostly for something to tell Roommate, and was three-quarters through without being impressed when he reached over and ate the leftover food off her plate. The gesture, somehow sexual, made all the difference.

Back in her car, he asked her middle name and she thought maybe he'd kiss her but instead he started coughing. Started arguing. Stupid things, God and what color the sky was. Joe believes in God just in case he might go to hell. She hadn't felt well. After dropping him off at his dorm, she was left with the runs and four hundred pages to read.

She's awake enough to do her essay if only there were light. Awake enough to want to go curse Joe out for keeping her up. In his letter, Timmy had written that all the guys were into NyQuil now. "It's incredible. Heroin addicts use it when they can't get a fix." Why did he say that? Why does he keep writing? It would be nice to see Timmy now. To just lie here with Timmy and not move and not say anything.

The door opens, no knock. Not Joe but Lars. For a second his hair glows from the hall light. With her eyes already adjusted to the dark, Alex can see Roommate sitting up, then pulling him down on the bed. What if Joe comes now? Then what?

She turns toward the wall. Hears the awful gasp "She's asleep" between kisses. Movie kisses that smack. Alex wants to get up but lacks a place to go except the library (probably closing) and Ponzio's room, where a girl is crying. But now it's too late to say she's awake. Bedspring and throat noise. It's too late to leave.

She moves closer to the wall. Zippers. Whispers. Lars's pants falling to the floor, pockets full of change. She wonders if his body is cold against Roommate's since he has poor circulation. She lies perfectly still and thinks how Lars cannot possibly see the makeup in the dark, then about makeup smeared on the pillowcase, then about her eye, which still itches. She hopes Roommate fucks up the oral report.

Thick breathing and giggle spurts. Bed squeaks have a rhythm, getting faster, and a tune, two highs and a low. Faster. Getting faster. Oh, faster. Washing over Alex, a warm tension—notes moving slowly up a scale. Lars on his saxophone groans deep, deep, deep like breath across empty bottles, yes. No! Control. Really so disgusting how Lars throttles that bed. Cheek on cold wall. Think essay, alarm clock, itchy eye, anything. But her hips want to move. Her hand wants to move.

There's a car light circling the room. There's a pillow jammed tight around her head. There's no Joe coming and she curls up, wondering just how tight her body can get.

6 | TILT-A-WHIRL

Ashtrays ignored, it's the Pub floor that's covered with butts. Flattened, soggy, and smoked way down. Alex gets three thirty-five an hour for sweeping them up with the big push broom. Better than the food pieces (some unrecognizable) or those impossible-to-sweep bits of paper, Styrofoam, plastic. Not nearly as good as the lost things—film canisters and pens, lighters, keys, textbooks, diet pills. Bad poems on napkins. Dollar bills.

Last night, someone's bra wrapped itself around a leg of the pinball machine. The night before, a real emerald earring and three perfectly rolled joints. She pocketed those and returned the earring, but the bra—that was a hard one. That she finally just left. It's enough trouble deciding whether to pick dimes from the dust pile without bothering about bras. Burn it? Keep it? Stand on a table in the cafeteria waving the thing, waiting for someone to claim it? She wonders if the girl will show up at the lost and found asking for it? Will the girl even notice it's gone?

Tonight, it's still here, collecting dust. Tonight, Alex finds a twelve-page paper by June Blackmore entitled "Van Gogh: The Lunatic/The Legend" and an empty tube of Sudden Tan.

It reminds her of summers spent working at Playland. In-spires her to put "Surfin' Safari" on the jukebox.

What a dumb song. She hopes no one passes by and sees her. She stops sweeping, leans on the broom and stares into nowhere.

How lonesome music from a party six, seven beaches down can sound. Even "Surfin' Safari." Parties at Camden are everywhere, all day. Just can't get that effect without distance. Music at Camden is everywhere, always. Just can't get that far away.

Except in the woods. For Alex, a new place. They have weeds that look like flowers, and real dirt, and the fall up here screams, glows, even smells. Trees are not puny, dis-eased things, they're climbable. Leaves hardly resemble the tannish sawdust balls at home.

It'd be hard to describe Camden to the people at home. Wilder than St. Patrick's Day in Rockaway and weirder than Catholic school. Coolness is newness is freakishness. Wear a tail. Tape your tits down. Bring some bugs up to lunch for your salad. And Alex, already different, does not have to try.

"Whatsamatter?" says Joe, startling her, pulling the broom from her hand. "Asleep standin up?"

"Oh . . . hi . . . nothing . . . no . . . I didn't hear you come in." She's unable to hold back a giant smile. The anthro-pology involved! Picture, for instance, Chowderhead in Camden.

"That glad to see me?"

"No—I mean yes—I mean no, no. I'm thinking." And still lost in herself she can't help laughing out loud. "Did I ever tell you about camp fire girls?"

"You were a—"

"No, these girls, they pile up their clutch bags and dance in circles around them. Ya know, like to make sure they're not stolen. My friend Peg calls 'em camp fire girls."

"You homesick?"

"Dontcha think that's funny?"

"I guess so. But what made you think of that?"

"What makes you think of anything?" Alex says, wishing she hadn't told him. He probably likes that kind of girl. Thinks the way their pumps sink into the sand is cute. But she tries again. Tells him a little about summer in Rockaway. The five-dollar Rockaway vacation: Take the A train. Buy some Night Train. Under the boardwalk, lodging with spectacular views and free seagull/calico crab dinner. ALL YOU CAN EAT. Again he doesn't get it, saying, "Summer in the city smells like old cat food."

She sweeps a mound of lipstick-pink cigarette filters from under the jukebox and leaves it in front of his feet. One girl smoked every one of them. You can tell by the color.

"Salmon," Joe says. "Maybe it was Dolores."

Dolores always has lipstick all over her face like she has no mirror.

"What I wanna know is how they got under there?"

"How does anything get anywhere?" mocks Joe, so infuriating right now.

She goes and puts money in the jukebox. Knows all the good numbers by heart. D7, "I'm on Fire," and F22, her current favorite: F22 for Tina singing the long version of "What's Love Got to Do with It." She'll have to make an effort not to sing along.

"Got any white-out?" asks Joe.

Of course. There has to be some reason he's here.

"Nope. But I got some Sudden Tan." She holds up the oily tube. "Maybe it's Dolores's."

"Well, it'd be real easy to pin that person. Shit turns ya orange im-mediately."

Alex throws the tube across the room, aiming for and

missing the trash can. So much for eight years of CYO basketball.

"I knew this girl," Joes goes on, "ate so many carrots her fingers turned orange."

June Blackmore at the window, pounding.

"It's here," Alex tells her, not giving her a chance to say anything.

June is bald, the latest, and wearing blue, not salmon, lipstick to make herself look dead. Passing the paper through the crack, Alex notices a newly chipped tooth. Slam dancing, no doubt.

"Oh God, thank God, thanks," June says. "Didya read it?"

"Just found it," Alex lies. "No."

"Oh, that's OK. Neither did I."

Alex is not entirely sure she's kidding.

"Joe? Is that Joe in there?" June blows kisses.

"Far as I can tell," says Joe. "You got any white-out?"

"Could be. Come with and we'll look."

Alex, acting disinterested, starts on the tables. She thinks about embarrassing June by telling her her bra was found wrapped around the pinball machine. But Joe might consider it a turn-on.

"I'll be over in a few," he says. "Thanks."

June points out the blackhead on Alex's nose.

"Dontcha have urges to squeeze those?" And she runs away, not another word.

Joe presses close against Alex's back, curls a wave of her hair on his index finger. She keeps scrubbing one very clean table.

"Does your friend Peg have a name for girls like June Blackmore?" he asks, obviously trying to ingratiate himself.

"Yeah," says Alex. "Assholes."

"I only asked for white-out."

"Did *I* say anything?"

But he's rubbing her neck, shit, licking her ear, shit, shit, Alex wondering what *would* Peg think of Camden girls? Girls like Roommate who iron their underwear, June Blackmore girls who don't wear underwear, wax their eyebrows, spacey girls with bells on their feet, militant feminists with serious muscle tone, girls who eat and throw up and eat. Girls like Alex has become. Kissing Joes who smell of other girls.

He pushes her gently against the wall, lifting her skirt with one hand, stroking her eyelids with the other.

"Yoohoo!" from June at the window. "Found some Correct-O-Type for you!"

Joe lets go. Turns. Doesn't seem the least bit upset, which Alex sure is. The slut doesn't even have the decency to say "Excuse me." Flings her Correct-O-Type through the window. Joe tries to catch, drops it.

"*Gracias,*" he says, but June runs off again, teasing.

Alex stands against the wall and watches as Joe takes a cigarette and matches from his pocket, puts the cigarette in his mouth and lights it, all with one hand. So smooth when he can't even catch.

"Well," she says. "Follow her if you want, I'm not gonna stop you."

"Gimme a break, Alex," he says, pushing a table and leaving. "Gimme a fuckin break."

Then, outside, leaning through the window, "Forget it. I'm sorry, OK? I gotta write this 'Psychology of Insects' shit. Whataya say to the cemetery later?" She shrugs and watches him walk away. Insects are Timmy's specialty. He has drawers crammed with bug books, magnifying glasses, jars. He escorts bugs outdoors and he still has an ant farm. But he's not good at walking away like Joe is.

"When I was in college," Alex's mother likes to say, "they couldn't come in our rooms. They paid for everything and wore ties." Her mother always calls men "they," just as she always calls the cleaning woman "the girl," even though she is forty-five.

Alex almost enjoys cleaning now. Cleaning thoroughly. She attacks the petrified chunks of gum and snot beneath tables, chanting "Blackmore, Blackheart." Removes slime from corners and under things she has to move or lift. "Baldhead, Blackhead." Places she's sure have never seen a sponge. All the frustration making her anal as hell, violent with the mop. At Playland she had to mop vomit from the Tilt-a-Whirl cars. June could make you vomit, with expressions like "yoohoo."

What her mother would say, "She'll get hers," is a lie. That wimpy, God-fearing idea that everything's even, or will be, one day. It's a lie Alex imagines she's scrubbing away. Till the Pub gleams. Floor so clean you can eat off it.

Her mother is having trouble with whatever it is she's trying to say. Alex, only amazed—what a coincidence. What are the odds she'd be thinking of her mother, walk in the dorm door to the phone ringing, answer it? What were the odds of her mother calling at all? Steep. She has to keep asking her to please speak up because some band is warming up in the basement.

"Alex dear, I've got news."

"I was just thinking of you. It's so weird, I was—"

"Listen, love, please."

"You OK?"

"Oh. Of course."

"Someone dead?"

"No. No, nothing like that."

"Well, what then?"

Her mother's nails gallop across a counter in Rockaway, or so Alex thinks. The band downstairs is whiny.

"What, Ma?"

"How should I put this?"

"How should I know? Just say it."

"We've rented out a room."

"You mean *my* room?"

Naturally. Where else? Then her mother really gets going. "Well, it's bills, dear, scholarship aside. We gave you that car and there's still room and board. Not to mention the book bills, the health plan, and—"

"It's OK. Sure. I understand."

And she does. That's the worst part. Her mother's been speaking without opening her mouth. Even over the phone you can tell. Only the lips move. Alex is good at smelling guilt.

Upstairs, Joe and his camera are outside her door. Apparently Roommate would not let him in. "He'd drool on my stuff and I'm trying to work." She's trying to work lying down, music blasting. And the only other thing she finds worth mentioning is the blackhead on Alex's nose.

It takes so much willpower not to say "Fuck off," but Alex says nothing, grabs a jacket, and goes. No room is her room, not this one or that one. No right to feel even the slightest self-pity. It's not like she studies, which might sort of justify. Assignments due weeks ago haven't been looked at. Joe is what's been looked at. Something due weeks ago. Or else why is she stamping through mud to a graveyard? Concentrate hard. Maybe he'll ask to take her picture.

The news that Joe is naked in the Pub comes to Alex via Roommate.

"It's loverboy and that Brazilian and this blubberman protesting the laundry machines going up to sixty cents. The three of 'em, on a table, NAKED!"

Alex does not know what to make of it. Roommate seems unduly excited, jumping on her bed to imitate.

"Inflation," she says in her lowest possible voice. "Ladies and gentlemen, are you prepared to pay one dollar and sixty cents to clean your clothes when you all well know a dollar sixty is three beers and change? A dollar sixty is *un*reasonable! We cannot afford—"

"All right, all right," says Alex. "I get the picture."

"Oh, no you don't. *You* didn't see 'em. They've got bow ties on and sneakers and they're like completely gone. C'mon, you're comin back with me. C'mon, I left Larry stranded."

The offer sounds hellish—being dragged to the Pub, where Joe is on a table naked, so that Roommate and Lars can make fun of her. But one of Alex's feet is asleep and she can't face rereading that same paragraph again, again not comprehending it. So she'll have a look. Too weird knowing that Roommate has seen Joe naked first. She'll go. Bring the book. Think it over.

In the book, these Indians go on a retreat. Take turns screwing a rock they believe was once some kind of goddess. Semipornographic. She also likes the part where the Hopi women pluck out their pubic hairs to give their lovers as souvenirs. But the whole thing is not that good. It goes on for five hundred pages. Ceremonial masks, the snake dance, sheep. Alex's paper is three weeks late.

They take the shortcut to the Pub, which means they walk across the grass. Alex is conscious of her legs moving.

Roommate says "You're walking funny" and "How was your *date* last night?" like ha ha, now he's in public naked.

"It wasn't a *date*," Alex says. "We went to a cemetery." She hates discussing anything with Roommate.

"I see, I see," says Roommate, flipping up her hair in the most annoying way.

But she doesn't see. Not anything. And it's absolutely no use. How can Alex even begin to tell her about Joe and his excuses? Teasing her, leaving her half-dressed. "My autonomy," "My math test," "That phone call I'm expecting." Roommate would think Alex was only protecting herself. For some reason Roommate *likes* to think that she and Joe have mad sex regularly but just don't want anyone to know.

In confession, as a child, Alex made up some wild lies. She thought her sins (not cleaning her room, not doing her homework) weren't good enough—bad enough—for God. And now she thinks of lying to Roommate. She could create the most elaborate scenario. She and Joe in the cemetery, in the all-night study room, in the back—oh, but who cares anymore.

On the Pub door someone has written "Sensory Deprivation Tank" in gold, metallic marker. Alex, still getting used to the way everyone usually turns to see who comes in, is thankful for the chaos inside. Tonight, no one's the least bit concerned.

"Forced to wear dirty underwear!" screams the naked Brazilian. "Do you call that justice?!"

He must've been up there an hour already by now.

"Do you like wearing dirty underwear?"

They spot Lars with his sax strap doing some kind of kar-

ate stretch against the wall. Acting all indifferent, not join-
ing in the crowd's shouts of "NO!"

"What did you say? I can't hear you."

"NO!" A regular rally, and Alex gets a glimpse of Joe then.
His permanent gummy smile—no indication of how he's
really feeling. He looks smaller without clothes and pale,
fidgety. Blubberman stands rigidly next to him, crimson.

"That's one dollar and sixty cents to wash and dry your
clothes."

"A dollar eighty," giggles Roommate. "You gotta run the
dryer twice."

Alex'd seen the guys in Rockaway naked plenty. Some
nights, twenty guys sliding through beer puddles, skinny-
dipping, jumping off bridges. But somehow this is different.
The amount of self-consciousness, maybe, or just plain lack
of skill at it.

"Take off your clothes while they're still nice and clean.
We mean business. One dollar and sixty cents can buy eight
boxes of macaroni and cheese. Feed four for a week."

Applause, but no one is cooperating. Alex prays Joe won't
speak, and is reminded of a very wasted girl, couple of weeks
ago, also on a table, saying she'd strip for five bucks. No one
would give it to her.

"One dollar and sixty cents does not include labor, trans-
portation, or detergent."

But the urgency is wearing off. People are getting bored.
The three stumble back down to the floor, the Brazilian and
Blubber exiting and Joe heading in the direction of the bath-
rooms.

"Cute ass," says Lars, poking Alex in the stomach, shaking
his head. "God, I would not be caught dead up there."

"Of course not," Alex wants to say. "You might start
twitching." But he's checking her out: "Congratulations, you
look very attractive tonight." Roommate already bitching

that she wants to leave. "So leave." With him. He doesn't wanna.

Alex leaves them alone to fight, buys herself two beers so she won't have to get up for a while. She knows she shouldn't stay but will. She knows she can't go before Joe reappears.

At a table in the corner, she pretends to read. The way the bouncer behind his magazine also pretends, fingering this month's *Field and Stream* as he watches the girls walk by.

At the next table sits a group of girls. Also an older woman (definitely someone's mother) chain-smoking Kents. Alex guesses the woman belongs to the girl in the clean shirt, who's chain-smoking Marlboros. Mother makes faces to indicate she doesn't like beer, doesn't like her daughter here with naked men. But she's trying. She moves awkwardly to the music. Olivia Newton-John singing "Let's Get Physical."

Olivia's really changed. She used to sing "I Honestly Love You" and wear white all the time. Maybe she's figured something out. Maybe she wasn't getting anywhere.

It occurs to Alex that she could've *made* Joe stay. Could've acted the way girls act. But seducer seems to her a role you stoop to. A role Olivia and Roommate and June Blackmore stoop to. And what *is* autonomy anyway? Mental note—look the word up in a dictionary.

Beginning the second beer, she imagines her own mother here. Impossible. Her own mother would have feigned tiredness. Gone back to the motel and done her nails, watched the news. It's sort of sad to think, but not as sad as this other mother, at the next table, drinking piss beer with her mink coat draped over a plastic folding chair.

They're discussing a story Daughter wrote "in an hour."

"What does it mean?"

"Should be longer."

"Why does she throw acid in his face?"

"Sounds to me like the cute parts in *The Waste Land*."

Alex does not understand, is nevertheless pleased by how distinctly she can make out their words in all the noise. Like distinguishing one voice from an entire chorus. Just by focusing, just by listening for it.

She experiments with other conversations. Girl lovers from her dorm talking sneakers. Green Sneakers got hers at Ames, cheap. Red Sneakers got hers from her sister, who "wore 'em for maybe three days."

Or, for a change, you can hear all the conversations in the room at once, a sound that crackles like cars driving on gravel. It's less work.

Her book drops to the floor on its own. Opens itself to the same goddamn paragraph. "I tried to castrate my males but did not have the heart for that; for I loved my sheep and knew the face of every one." Makes perfect sense. What's the big deal? She even likes that about the faces, picks up the book to underline. But her hand underlines, really. As soon as she sees Joe approaching, she watches her hand underline.

Groin at eye level. He leans over, a kiss? Sweet from the two packs of gum he chews daily since he quit smoking. Ashy from starting again. Now he smokes and chews simultaneously.

"Well," he says. His glasses are crooked and he's got that dumb smile—he's obviously smashed. Holding a pitcher of beer, no cups.

"Well," she repeats, deciding to concentrate on his bow tie, certain that everyone's watching. Sure that Roommate and Lars have abandoned their fight to watch.

"Congratulations," she hears herself saying. "You look very attractive tonight."

He bangs the pitcher down. "All right! Sorry to embarrass you. Don't think this was my idea."

He could've at least thought it up if he was gonna go

through with it. What is she doing here, listening to this? Confused account of his evening in town. Camden crowd found a salad bar back in some alley. Got thrown out stealing croutons or cherry tomatoes or something. Joe started a fight.

Whatever that has to do with the laundry machines remains a mystery. He wants to show her the bruise above his eye.

"Look," Alex says, "if you haveta talk to me at least sit down."

"Thought you'd never ask."

She can't see any bruise above his eye, but she can hear him better. Some townie guy was making fun of them, said "Dress 'em up, send 'em to college," wounding insult to someone as stylish as Joe.

"Aren't you freezing?"

"No."

He takes the pen from her book and starts writing on her arm. It annoys, vaguely excites her. They look at each other, then down at the table, then back at each other the way Alex used to do with boys in junior high.

It looks like the pen has exploded on her arm. Once in junior high a pen exploded in her mouth. Extreme humiliation and black ink on her teeth for weeks.

He appears to like that story. Makes an adorable face, then spits in his hand and tries to rub the writing off. But it won't come off, only blurs, and he's rubbing too hard.

"Why'd ya do that?" she snaps, retracting her arm.

"I don't know."

"Why'd ya put spit on me?"

"I wish you smoked," says Joe. "I couldn't carry cigarettes, no pockets."

That makes her instantly like him again.

"Just don't get up, I'll ask someone." She goes over to the

next table where Mother is pulling tissues from her sleeve to wipe up spilt beer. Asks in general and very politely if anyone can spare a cigarette.

They all look at her, motionless. Another try. Again, very politely. This time an anorexic blonde with paint on her face points to a pack of Camels. Alex assumes this means "Take one" and she watches them all watch her do it. Thanks. Thanks a lot.

"Filterless," Joe says. "Hardcore. But I need a light."

"Well, forget it. I'm not goin back there." Then, afraid he'll stand up, "Neither are you. We'll just wait and ask someone walking by."

"I gotta get up eventually."

"Not till I'm gone."

"A little uptight?"

"Shut up."

"Making you tense?"

"I said shut up."

She looks away. Plays her focus game.

Red Sneakers: "What nationality are your parents?"

Green Sneakers: "European."

Green and Red Sneakers both stare at the mother at the next table.

"OK," says Joe. "I'm sorry, OK?" He rips apart Alex's plastic cup. "I think I'm meeting someone else here."

"You think?"

"Well, the plans were sort of—"

"Naked?"

"That part just came up."

"So."

"So nothing. I thought you should know."

"Is that what you're savin all this beer for?"

"I just don't think—"

"It doesn't matter."

"Alex, you're so nice and—"

"I said it doesn't matter."

"I need someone who'll like grab me under the table or something—you're just too nice."

"I'm getting cups."

"See, you're nice. Could you get me some matches while you're up?"

"I am not nice."

"You are."

"I'm not and I'm not gettin you any fuckin matches."

Nice? Timmy had never accused her of that. No one had. Could she ever grab someone under the table? And why, why isn't she able to think of a good comeback on the spot, instead of later, brushing her teeth, in bed, or after hearing what Roommate would have said?

Her mother likes to tell her she's lucky. "Your generation, girls go after what they want and get it. *We* waited by the phone." But Alex's mother would not be encouraging her to go after what she wanted if she knew what it was. And, thinking of her mother, Alex cannot grab him. She gets cups. Tries again to read what he wrote on her arm. Pink arm still, from the rubbing. She can see just one letter—B. But it's OK. This way, it can say anything she'd like.

Roommate runs up. Exaggerated delight.

"Really," she says, "you should strip. Make him feel more comfy. Didya notice the mole by his hip?" Followed by a fit of fake laughter. Her laughter is like a bad smell Alex has to get away from. Back to Joe? Oh, just go home. But her book is still there. Joe is reading her book.

"I tried to castrate my males," Alex recites, "but did not have the heart for that."

"You're good, Alex . . . a lot. Do you know what time it is? Around? I got a toothache."

"You're drunk," she says, pouring herself more beer.

"She'll be here any minute."

"Who?"

"The person I'm meeting."

"June Blackmore?"

"I thought it didn't matter."

"It doesn't."

Alex and the bouncer exchange frowns. He's frowning but dancing in his chair, which looks odd since he's not moving in synch to "Dare to Be Stupid" on the jukebox but to something else, who knows what, on his Walkman. She stares at her hand through the beer, through the plastic cup. It looks swollen.

"I'm flirting with five people," Joe says, "and not really following through with any of it."

"Not really?"

"Well, she's gonna be—"

"Here any minute. What if all five were gonna be here any minute?"

"That'd be a challenge."

"Yeah. That'd really be takin your ego out for an ice cream."

Alex's mother once came back from Waldbaum's and discovered the back of her pants unzipped. She'd been walking around in Waldbaum's, speaking to women she knew, buying things, loading the car, all with her pants unzipped. It was terrible. Alex laughed and laughed. She fell on the floor laughing.

But now, walking away from the Pub with her book, she

understands. She feels as if her pants have been unzipped in Waldbaum's, only worse. Like she knew her pants were unzipped and for some reason didn't fix them.

TV noise through Ponzio's door. "The Essence of Shaving."

"Come in! Come in!" he yells psychically, before she knocks. But it's locked, so she waits for him to open it.

Dorm's haunted, he insists. Door locks itself. Alarm clocks float above desks. He plays chess with an invisible opponent.

"Ya think I turned on the TV? Ya think I have any control over my appliances whatsoever?"

Yes, this is the right place to be. Time to finally fix her pants.

She suggests going to the cemetery. "Spook ourselves out."

"You want spooky?" he says, pointing to the TV. "Chicken McNuggets are injected with chicken skin fat, then deep fried in beef shortening."

"Seagull McNuggets," says Alex, a Rockaway reference not worth explaining.

He picks what appears to be a lint ball off her sweater. This wonderful expression—mock worry—flashes on his face. Playing at playing Ponzio, Big Brother. Then Ponzio, Oracle Senior. "Beware of smiley men unusually interested in graveyards."

Of course he knows all about Joe. Through the wall. Or from Roommate. He probably knows gossip about Alex she hasn't heard yet. But it's fine, she's not even surprised. It's a sign that she's assimilating.

"We can watch the sunrise."

"It's ten-thirty, Alex."

"Well, I don't know." She sits on a crate. "Graveyards aren't too scary with Joe. He takes photos. Tells all the spirits to wave for the camera."

Ponzio only nods. The phone rings. Neither of them moves. "Shalimar," says the TV. "The perfume that comes as close to forever as a perfume can."

"That doesn't mean anything," Alex says. "Gimme the Jim Beam I see sticking out from that pile of dirty clothes."

Starting to tell him about the Pub, she figures he already knows. Instead, "Do you think I'm nice?"

"Nice? Sure."

"Oh, shit."

A hidden talent. Ponzio can play the spoons. He shows Alex the calluses on his pale thighs. Then, demonstrating, legs, spoons, hands blur, and his tongue dangles out without him knowing it.

Alex decides it's impossible to drink lying down. If Ponzio'd slow down she could tell him stuff. Her room is rented out. June Blackmore is a bitch. The Hopis believe that owls turn to witches in the dark and throw stones. But she doesn't really want to tell him any of it, clacking away over there in his tight little boxer shorts. She has something else to say.

"Ponzio?"

He nods.

"I'm gonna tell you a story. You don't haveta talk, OK?"

He nods again and the spoons chatter double time.

"The last time I worked at Playland—this was maybe two, three summers ago—the last *night* at Playland . . . Did I already tell you this story?"

Ponzio shakes his head.

"So, regular boring night at work. Peg, my friend, is there just hanging out. Tilt-a-Whirl, I'm positive. Anyway, these two Brooklyn girls come stomping over, ya know, spike heels, tube tops, totally greasy from the beach. And they're standing there arguing over whether or not to get on, right? So the blond one, she was obviously the leader—she had sunglasses on her head—she asks Peg what she thinks she's starin at, and Peg says, 'Get on, if you're gonna stand there.' I'll never forget this. And the girl says, 'I *axed* you a question.' And Peg says, 'I know what I'm staring at.' 'Yeah, what?' 'Slime. Slug slime from across the bridge.' So the girl starts pushing at Peg, pulling on her braid, and the other girl's going, 'This place is sooo beat, Dar*leen*,' so *I* tell her, 'Go home.' "

Ponzio's tapping has lost all its rhythm.

"Before I know it we're like paired off, fighting. Mighta been my first real fight, and *my* girl is this little Italian animal, I mean biting and spitting, besides the fact that she was so fucking slippery. But the funniest thing—she held on to this *reflector* the whole time. Like it was her boyfriend or something. And by this time we've got a crowd around us and my boss comes running to break it up."

Ponzio has stopped beating completely. He leans forward on his chair, letting the spoons fall off his legs. Alex, pleased with the attention, passes him the Jim Beam.

"Dar*leen* acts all pouty and sexy to my boss, this *sleazy* guy, saying, 'Lookit. She broke my sunglasses in half.' And my boss is just starin at her tits and sniveling. And what really got me, after all that, he lets 'em on for *free*! Peg was like beyond pissed. Kicking everything and screaming about how she was gonna strangle the bitch with her own belly chain. Turns out this Dar*leen* ripped a whole clump of Peg's hair out."

"Wow," Ponzio says, "really? What happened to you?"

"A couple big bruises. *My* girl used her shoes."

"Then what?"

"Well, I couldn't let this thing continue. I didn't know what Peg would do, so I said I was sick of the job anyhow, only partly true, and why not just leave 'em up there, spinning till the park closed? Probably no one would find them till the park closed and that was hours away. They'd be puking cotton candy all over each other by then."

"Yeah!" Ponzio says. "Way to go!" And he kisses Alex's wrist, "for her brains," he says.

They decide to go back to the Pub. Alex realizes she's got to clean up all over again and she needs incentive—fresh anger and more beer. The Jim Beam has given her the illusion she's thinking clearly. She'll write her paper tomorrow on the Hopi idea that all disease is from worry left to harden in your stomach.

They run into Roommate and Lars, who are just now leaving. Without having to ask, Alex hears all the info. Joe *did* meet "this bald girl" and they left half an hour ago. Roommate's tone implying that Alex blew it again.

"What is wrong with that chick?" asks Ponzio when they're inside. "Is she just plain evil or sick in the brain?"

"Is there a difference?" But Alex doesn't want him to answer and goes on to explain the Hopi worry cures. Drinking urine or warm water or tickling the neck with buzzard feathers.

They toast to it. They toast to everything, taking turns. Lars's twitch. Championship spoon jamming. June's cold bald head. Papers and theses, tombstones, pets, the month of November. Then Alex, with a special toast to her old boss whose breath always smelled like the bottom of a popcorn cup. And finally to Dar*leen* and her friend, still twirling, even with the park closed for the winter, the two of 'em still whirling around, green as could be. June is conveniently superimposed on the image of the little Italian in Alex's mind.

"Thing is," she says, cup raised higher than ever, "you can't get even but you *can* get revenge."

And then something strange follows that thought in her head.

It's different here. On your own, sure, you can do anything. But same as home, you sit in a bar instead.

VACATION | 7

It's all decided. Joe will stay in Rockaway overnight and fly out of Kennedy in the morning, early, and be in California for Christmas.

After introductions, after dinner, after offering to do the dishes, she'll take him out on the empty beach with the dog and show him how hard the sand gets. So hard you can walk on top without leaving a footprint. Then peppermint schnapps or wine or whatever they find in her parents' cabinet to pass back and forth in the sand wind. And maybe one of those sunsets, red and oozing, that only chemicals can make. And maybe snow.

It'll be snowing and they'll realize it's Christmas Eve and that only means a reason for—but no. She cannot think about that. "Maybe" sucks. She cannot expect a thing.

Alex is thirsty, goes up to the cafeteria. Until the food line she does not even realize that in half a year at Camden this is her first time at breakfast. Relatively slight hangover from the Santa Clothes party (peppermint schnapps), but there's a lot that seems erased: her money, for one, then how she got this gash in her leg, how she got home, undressed, in bed.

Hard-boiled eggs look plastic in the long metal tray. She hates hot hard-boiled eggs, decides on toast. Plenty of time to think and look around by the toaster. All these people who probably go to breakfast every day. She never knew. Some are wearing sunglasses, a good idea. Some, pajama tops. Some are even eating salad. Imagine, salad for breakfast.

She drinks four glasses of grapefruit juice as she stands by the toaster, letting the bread go through twice, and looks for Joe's red jacket. Finally she sits down with Ponzio and that girl in her Social Anthro class with the beret. They look embarrassed, and Alex figures they must've slept together. Must've woken up surprised to see each other. It is possible, perhaps, to find out who everyone slept with. Just by watching who they come in with. Another feature of breakfast she's been missing all along.

"Alex at breakfast!" Ponzio says. "Holy shit!"

"I wanna leave early. I wanna get the hell outta here."

"New York?" asks Alberta.

Alex is pretty sure that's her name. "Well, right outside—Rockaway."

"*You* know," Ponzio tells her, "The Ramones—'Rock, rock, Rockaway Beach.' " He pounds his spike bracelet into a pile of napkins.

"Yeah," Alex says, "claim to fame." She has always suspected the Ramones just used the name without ever going there.

"Neat," says Alberta, probably assuming Alex knows them personally.

They talk about the Ramones' new album, their Social Anthro teacher's toupee, and Christmas. Christmas gets Alberta and Ponzio into a fight, since she's a Jehovah's Witness and he's nothing. Thinks Jehovah's Witnesses have "some nerve," bothering people on the street and at their doors.

When Alberta starts in on the Second Coming, Alex excuses herself.

Poor Ponzio. He didn't know what he was getting himself into last night. Drunk, horny, with that pathetic Santa beard she saw him make out of cotton balls in the bathroom. Poor Alberta, having to feel obligated to God that way, like an employee.

Not Alex. Outside in the sun, real cold, there she feels free. At least hangover free. Maybe she'll go to breakfast all the time. Running back to the dorm through a trail of snow that someone has dyed pink and blue, she wonders whether it's true that Joe kissed her last night, by the speaker, or if she dreamed it.

Roommate's snoring. A little sick from standing outside in her socks, arguing with Lars. A little hot probably now, with all her clothes still on. One of her earrings is missing.

Alex packs silently, all the old favorites plus the sweater her mother made. She thinks about the drive. They can sing, stop for lunch, anything. And she thinks of her parents, hoping Joe will shave for their sake. Hoping he'll act smart and not smoke and offer to do the dishes for their sake.

She wants to wake her roommate to say goodbye, have a nice vacation, say how excited she is, how she's sorry for calling Lars a geek last night. That she was just drunk and sort of lonely but now everything's fine. Everything's just fine.

Instead, she reopens the suitcase, changes into the sweater her mother made (it isn't that bad), and writes a note that says nothing. Not a word about how much she likes her roommate right now, asleep. The way you can really like a sleeping person, it's funny.

See you in a couple of weeks. Have fun skiing. Remember heavy socks, preferably wool, and gloves at all times.

Agree to no Suzy Chapstick–type TV spots. A souvenir would be nice. One of those landscape bubbles that snow when you shake them. Joy to the world. The Lord has come. From Alex.

On her way out, Alex trips over the hot plate, uncovering—oh yeah, last night—the lists, all the guys they'd ever slept with. It's quite a complex graph, numbered and tallied. Roommate's half has lots of cross-outs and cryptic little asterisks and arrows. There are, thank God, no overlaps.

Roommate sneezes in her sleep and mumbles something that sounds German. Alex is now certain that some of her money was lost right here, betting. Roommate's list obviously won by a landslide with five no-namers, just "French guy" or "Rob's friend from NYU," like that.

Alex puts the lists down and changes back to her original shirt. By the time she's done that and then packed the car, Roommate's alert and burning the lists in the hot plate.

"You were hoping they'd self-destruct?" asks Alex, trying to be funny, searching the room for the comb she forgot.

"Safe home" is all Roommate says. She does not look up.

To brace herself, Alex stops and parks for a minute before driving the last block home. Six kids are playing TV tag in the street, naming shows she doesn't recognize. She talks. How can going seventy feel static when parked here, it's like she's whipping forward fast? Joe doesn't know. He "needs coffee." At last they're here and he cannot understand what she's waiting for.

A fog collects or it just gets darker. No telling with the clock stuck at six a.m. At six a.m. they were still up partying, which could have something to do with Alex's illusion that the kids are shrinking.

Step on a crack, they're crying now. Break your mother's back. Step on a line/Break her spine. It's the volume, not the rhyme, that makes Alex nervous. When she starts up the car, the children glide sideways, slow motion, and go one at a time through a hedge. The car seems to take up the whole street.

At the side door, she expects the dog, Scrapy, to greet them, but no, and—what's that smell? Noodles? Perfume? She's strangely aware of how soon it will go. How soon smells disappear once you get inside them.

She's standing in *her* hall with Joe, in between two blobs of white dissolving carpet cleaner. Voices from the kitchen sound so high and lubricated, like the Chipmunks, that she goes on, closer, closer, till she's standing in the doorway.

"May lightning strike me if I ever heard any such thing about Hal Shark!" It's her mother. And Dad, "I told you not five minutes ago!" Though the fighting's familiar, the name, Shark, is not, and she looks at Joe as if he could explain. But he's plainly annoyed that Alex is not going in, sighs and sticks a piece of gum in his thin face. And just when she's thinking how rare it is, how almost nice it is to see Joe not smiling for once, Dad begins to giggle.

He giggles a lot for a fifty-two-year-old man. He drops his head back and sputters like a machine gun. Then, suddenly seeing her in the doorway, he stops, runs over, and squeezes her neck.

"The Ghost of Christmas Past!" he beams.

Alex feels dumb wanting to kiss him, asks, "How've ya been?" She sets her suitcase down. "This is my friend Joe." She realizes she misses him. For the first time, misses her dad when he is right here.

"How do you do, son?" extending his arm, triple the thickness of Joe's. "Come in, come in. Merry Xmas."

"And to you."

Alex marvels at how calm Joe is and wonders what new side of him will come through in Rockaway.

"You're home!" shouts her mother as if she hasn't noticed till now. She slaps her leg with a dish towel, kisses at the air, and says, "You didn't disturb the carpet cleaner, now?" Then, smiling at Joe, she offers coffee.

"How's the driving?" Dad wants to know.

"Good."

"Any problems with the car?"

"No."

"Anything I should know about?"

"No."

And with that taken care of, her parents return to their chores. Everything resumes except the argument about Hal Shark.

Alex and Joe set out to look for Scrapy, who's apparently ill from eating sand. She knows Joe's thinking of the pet cemetery where they stopped on the drive down, a find that made him momentarily ecstatic. Oh, he's definitely thinking about it, such a wicked smile when he sees Scrapy laid out flat on the dining room tiles. He's just itching to develop that film.

But it's *her* Scrapy, and he can hardly lift his snout, so ancient and bland that Alex wants to shout at Joe, Stop thinking what I know you're thinking. The sign said "Resting Place for Man's Best Friend. Complete Funeral Services with Human Dignity. Non-biodegradable Caskets. Burials 7 Days and Holidays." Oh, it was plush all right. Poor Scrapy would only get buried in the backyard, in cardboard. And Joe does not want to go walk him on the beach *or* play cards *or* watch TV. After three cups of coffee, he finds a couch.

. . .

Alex watches Dad wind clocks, her mother peel carrots. The latter gesture is a little like the circling of the Brazilian's hand when he can't locate a precise word or phrase in English.

"He seems like a nice boy. Not lots to say, but bright. Must be plain worn-out." Alex is about to say something stupid when her father lets out another giggle.

"She thinks he's wearing a girl's shirt."

"Just stop, Frank. I never said any such thing."

The phone rings.

"Oh!" Dad says. "Timmy called. I forgot. How is he?"

"*You* spoke to him, not me."

"I like Timmy. I like that boy."

"I know."

One of the only things Alex and her mother had ever agreed upon was the decision to stop seeing Timmy. She calls him "hooligan." But Dad was a lifeguard himself once and, whether from loyalty or simply a passion for swimming, he thinks Timmy's great. Needs a father (-in-law?) is all. He's sure she will come to her senses and make up with him. Only, he worries. By then, who knows, it may be too late.

"I fixed his brakes down at the garage for nothin," Dad says. "Not a bad little car he's got there."

"Yeah."

Alex hears her mother say into the phone, "I keep a jar full of fingernails on the windowsill. When one breaks, I just glue another on in a jiffy." She actually says that. Dad, who apparently heard it too, looks confused. What windowsill? Can there be some windowsill he doesn't know about?

"I been tricked," he says, one giggle. "All this time, I really thought they were hers."

When her mother gets off the phone they both stare at her hands, at the thin lines where the nails are adhered. Weird.

"Are they plastic? Are they polished? I mean, *in* the jar?"

"Well, either. Usually I get the natural, then polish them myself. More variety." She seems pleased with Alex's interest.

"On or off?" asks Dad.

"On, obviously."

With him she's not pleased. Abruptly, she turns away, switches on the weather (fog) on the tiny Sony.

"Who's Hal Shark?" Alex remembers to ask.

"Your mother is going senile. Forgets everything I tell her in five minutes."

Alex's mother heaves and opens something with the electric can opener. It's as if she needs to create some new noise each time she gets irritated. Now, with all her sources used up, she apparently figures her voice will do.

"IT'S LIKE THAT QUEENSBOROUGH BRIDGE THING ALL OVER AGAIN!"

Alex is without a clue as to what's going on.

"What Queensborough Bridge thing?"

She's afraid her mother might start vacuuming or something.

"This creep called up wanting money. Said I smashed into his car on the Queensborough Bridge."

"And—"

"And *your* father keeps telling me maybe I hit him and forgot. Can you believe that? HIT HIM AND FORGOT!"

Dad looks bored, sort of whines, "For the billionth time, Dorothy, he knew our names, the car, other things. Anyway, I was only checking."

"DO YOU FORGET *your* CAR ACCIDENTS?"

Her mother furiously wipes exploded food from the microwave.

"What in God's name does that have to do with your Hal, tell me?"

Your Hal? By now, Alex is thoroughly lost. "Is Hal the bridge man?" But no one is answering. "Well?"

"No. No, he's someone else," her mother says softly.

It's all too ominous.

"For chrissakes, Dorothy, tell her."

"The boarder. Alex, we *did* explain to you about the boarder."

Yes. And Alex had prepared herself for it. Only . . . only she'd overlooked one simple fact. It isn't just subtraction—*her* room, taken away. Addition is also involved. There is a *real* person with a name, belongings, a life. And so on top of everything else, Alex has to deal with how moronic she feels.

She walks over to the window. She knows this view so well from memory that she can see even what the fog blocks out. Particularly the bird weathervane on the garage roof, its beak permanently open in song or retching, depending on your mood.

She wonders whether Hal Shark screws in her bed, a crude thing to wonder first. And then whether her mother changes his sheets regularly, like in a hotel.

"Where's he now?" Her third thought.

"In Miami," says Dad. "Watching his mother die."

The statement sends some utensil flying out of her mother's hand. Again she's insisting that she has not heard this information before.

Three explosions. From somewhere outdoors. A pause. Then two more.

"Firecrackers?" her mother says. "Still? In December? Doesn't anyone remember it's Christmas Eve? I can't believe those godawful kids haven't been called in yet!"

You can hear them outside—thrilled into shouting by the noise. *Why?* No sparks or colors, just noise. Alex wonders if it's the same kids she saw earlier. She can't see anything now. Fog, an aluminum wall. She leans far enough out the window to fall easily, but she still can't see anything.

Her mother is watching TV again. News and weather have turned into a game show. Just let *her* go on one of those programs, she'd be rich. How often she says so. Though her eyes are fixed on the screen, she's simultaneously swishing cutlets at ninety-degree angles in a bowl of egg yolks. Her shoulders so pulled back that it makes Alex uncomfortable. Name a vegetable you chop. And the woman says, "Hamburgers."

"Hamburgers! What an asshole." But her mother only makes her neck crooked. Alex thinks of Ponzio buying burgers at McDonald's and not eating the burger part. Throwing the burger part out the window since he likes just the buns with the goop on them.

"Chop, chop, chop meat," sings Dad, dragging a chair around that he stands on to reach the higher clocks. It's quite important that he keep his clocks as synchronized as possible. Not easy; he's got ninety-five clocks, ninety-six when he opens his gift.

"Do something nice with your hair," her mother says during the commercial. "You've got company."

"He's passed out."

"How about pinning it up? Get the brush, I'll do it for you."

Alex doesn't move.

"Don't you want to look nice, even for your old parents?"

"You're not old," Alex says, noticing a strand of gray in her mother's black hair. Like tinsel. Hard to believe it's been there all this time, without Alex seeing it.

Dad kind of squeals and abandons his chair to take Alex's hand. He pinches a piece of skin near her wrist and holds it up.

"Watch how quick it jumps back," he says, letting go. It

mother punched your mother right in the nose. What color blood came *out?*

She has herself all set up for a good cry when Joe appears in the doorway. She has, surprisingly enough, forgotten about him.

"They told me you'd be down here," he says, "but they didn't tell me that you hang out in closets, in the dark." She can't help talking to him, complaining to him about her room, her mother, Hal Shark.

"That's not so bad. My parents took in this lunatic wetback with like two teeth left. Hasn't paid a cent of rent, but they think it's funny listening to him struggle with English."

How badly *do* her parents need the money?

"He's been chewin tobacco since he was nine or somethin," Joe goes on. "I know he's gonna get mouth cancer."

He does not answer when Alex asks what he thinks of her parents, when Alex asks is she selfish, is she childish, does her hair look all right? He lights a cigarette and smiles and makes it quite clear that he does not want to get involved.

Upstairs, the house has evolved into Christmas. Which means the tree's plugged in, her parents are pushing eggnog. Fog has broken into a hard rain.

"I'm dreaming of a wet Christmas," sings Dad, sort of waltzing. Joe asks for a beer.

"Your parents must be sad, you not being home tonight," says her mother, who had done up her dark hair in a very severe sort of French twist. She's wearing a heavy watch around her neck, on a chain. For Dad, Alex hopes, as only that motive will allow her to overlook the ridiculous way it separates her mother's bosom.

"It's OK," says Joe. "They're atheists."

Alex remembers school: Ponzio and his Jehovah's Witness. And how June Blackmore, that Jap, always walks around saying she's Buddhist.

For a change, this year, the theme is red alone. Red bulbs on the tree and red paper flowers, actually nice. Is it red that makes you hungry? She pokes holes in a napkin with her fork.

"Forgot the trouble, that's the trouble with our love" is playing on the radio, so scratchy it sounds hiccoughed. Alex isn't sure why everyone looks larger than before.

Joe appears to be perfectly comfortable here. Lounging even. All Joe needs is a beer and he's perfectly comfortable. Her mother definitely approves of him, although her reasons are unclear. She moves closer to him on the couch. A warm voice for the questioning. She pokes for information about Camden, about what she calls "the social scene." The ratio, the type of activities, and, for some reason, the number of gays. She sniffs at her drink (Fresca and gin, always) and plays with the watch necklace and generally drives Alex crazy, saying she hopes Alex is behaving herself up there, saying what she wouldn't do to be a carefree college student again. She strokes the couch with long peach fingernails.

Alex is certain that her mother will not like the blouse she's getting for Christmas. And vice versa. But it won't make a difference, which, in a way, is worse. It doesn't take all that much to please her mother: neatness and beige. And if for once Alex could leave the wrapping intact, salvageable, when she opens a gift. It seems easy enough in theory, but, like Dad, Alex can't do it really. Christmas wears out, it seems, without kids, without some kind of mystery.

Even Timmy's house, sick as it is, must be filled right now with incredible hope. "O Come All Ye Faithful," so touchingly tone-deaf. Joyful and triumphant. While here Christmas is more like something you *get through*. While here Joe is telling his joke. A memory? As a kid he used to think lesbians were just ugly girls.

Alex remembers young Scrapy yapping in time to the blinking tree lights. She almost has an urge to pray. She feels sort of sorry for Hal Shark with his mother dying and his two shoehorns. What did he need two for? And what would Joe say if she suggested midnight Mass?

Dad announces it's begun to snow. Her mother pays no attention, still busy interrogating Joe. What do his parents do? What does *he* want to do? Does he know Alexandra is on scholarship? Is he through with California or is the East too cold, too damp? What time is the flight home? And where did he get that unusual shirt?

Although Alex wishes she'd stop already, attend to the food, she also wishes that Joe wasn't so loose, answering with whatever happens into his head—like what the fuck, I'll probably never see these people again. Still, her mother is amused, charmed even. Maybe she and Alex have more in common than it seems. Or less. Oh, you might say Joe's elusive if he wasn't so vain. You might say he's smooth if he wasn't so strange.

He thinks he'll choke.

When she walks in, is walking in and straight toward him, Timmy swallows an ice cube and thinks he'll choke. Definitely can't speak, frozen throat. And Alex right here, snow on her eyelashes.

"Hey, Timmy," she says, and kisses him, shit, while his head's moving. It lands somewhere near his ear. Please rewind. It's supposed to be different from this.

Alex just talks up a storm. This strand of tinsel she obviously doesn't know about is attached to her elbow.

"Oh," Timmy thinks. That's all he can think. Then he has a coughing fit.

"You all right? Drink something. Give the signal, I'll Heimlich. You drunk? What should I drink? Beer? Or a real drink? How's your mother and Agnes? Where's Chowder? Merry Christmas." And other things Timmy can't hear on top of his own coughing. The way coughing or crying fills up your whole head.

Later, he'll hit himself. Taking fifteen minutes to realize she isn't alone. Some guy in a girl's shirt hands her a drink and she touches his arm, *lightly*, says she'll buy the next. NEXT? It's enough to bring Timmy's voice back.

"Introduce me to your friend."

Alex stands there. Her damp, wavy hair fits so nicely behind her small ears—real seductive.

"Joe," the guy says, creepy smile and weird accent. "Hi, mah name's Joe."

"Oh, yeah?" Timmy says, happy how mean he sounds. But seeing it in her face, you asshole, he immediately reconsiders.

Chowderhead would want to beat the guy's face in. And Sloane probably would. But Timmy, who never understood about that stuff anyway, is just embarrassed.

Thing is, it might be fun, but only briefly. Alex would surely leave. Whether he beats or is beaten, Joe will have won and everyone will have seen Timmy's dumb old bruise that won't heal, that refuses to heal, just turns colors, aches on occasion. This occasion. And Joe will be just one more guy Timmy has stuck his fist into.

Not this time. Finally someone to hate and he's gonna get to know him. Act big, free drinks and the buddy system. Because it's no use hating Alex, Timmy's tried.

Staring at Joe slurp his wimp drink, Seven and Seven, Timmy works at memorizing the image. It'll come in handy sometime, playing rugby or later, walking home, when the trees start getting sexual the way they do. White collecting in the crevices. Miserable Timmy will picture Joe knocking back Seagram's and making like he's playing the guitar. Special emphasis on the upbeats of "Miss Me Blind." Boy George, the fem, it figures.

"Where ya from?" Timmy asks, completely new voice, new face, and he even grins, holding out some darts to Joe. A little friendly competition? Alex smiles too, can't help it. And she can smile, man, with a mouth that once appeared on the cover of *Orthodontia Monthly.*

"California," Joe says, missing the dart board. Ha ha. "San Diego."

Timmy's seen pictures in *Surfer* magazine. He's jealous as hell. This guy doesn't surf, though, he can tell. Too skinny.

"Do any surfing?" he asks anyhow.

"No way. Seen too many people fucked up."

"Fucked up?"

"Ya know, paralyzed and shit."

Pleasant. Pleasant dude. Looks like young Dick Van Dyke with bad skin and glasses. And it's only ten-thirty.

Already ten-thirty and nothing. No touch, not even a look. Alex had done better at school. And doesn't it humiliate him to be losing his second game of darts to Timmy? She could kill herself for caring and kill her mother for all those ridiculous "under the mistletoe" hints. Boys don't think that way, Ma, don't you know?

She sits at a table, watching the game, clasping a swizzle stick between pinky and thumb. If it bends in the middle, that means luck. If it doesn't, well, what if it doesn't? Forget it.

"Go on," says a voice. Peg's hoarse voice from behind her. "Let's see, you gonna get lucky or what?"

As Alex turns to say hi, three candy canes drop in her lap.

"Merry Christmas!" Peg's nose is running. "Let's drive out to Howard Beach and check out those mega nativity sets."

"Aren't you gonna ask how I am first?"

"I can see—you're overtired, depressed, slightly drunk, and glad there's me," Peg says, messing up Alex's hair. "So there." She marches over to the dart game, where she kisses Timmy's forehead and demands to be introduced to "the handsome stranger." That makes Alex happy.

"Alex's friend," Timmy said, letting loose a dart aimed for nowhere. He's lucky it lands in a plant and lucky Sloane's bartending and likes that kind of shit.

"Watch it, Ray!" Sloane howls. "Some nice ass around here that we don't wanna puncture!"

Peg spins on the heel of her boot, and Alex thinks she's going to yell something back. But she only gives Sloane a dirty look, mutters "Smack," and then checks out Joe.

"Alex's friend? *So*, when did this happen?"

Not waiting for an answer, she skips back over to the table and sits down.

"He's got such shiny hair," she whispers. "But he can't play darts for shit."

"It's not what you think. He'll probably hit on *you*. It's really not what you think."

Peg just laughs. "I don't think. *You* think. That's how come you got a scholarship. But it's vacation, and you're supposed to stop thinking already. Start partying."

"I partied a lot up there," Alex tells her. "I partied a lot last night." She rolls up her pants to show off the mysterious gash, really just a scrape.

"I'd like to scrape Sloane's face off," Peg says so loudly that Timmy turns and nods. His sad eyes look yellowish.

"I was thinkin the same thing," he says. "I was thinkin how him and Bean used to hold me down, breathe in my face till I guessed what they ate. I was just tellin Joe that."

Timmy's got this amazing memory but seems to remember mostly things worth forgetting.

"I can't believe *your* mother let you out on Christmas Eve," Peg says to him. She's wincing, trying to untangle a large, yellow knot of hair.

"I'm nineteen."

So, last year you were eighteen."

"Good math."

"So last year you weren't out."

"Good memory."

"I quit smoking pot."

"Did not."

"Did too. Well, sort of."

"Last year," Timmy says, by now standing over the table, "I was working. No, that was New Year's. Last year, oh yeah, I got bombed and fell asleep at midnight Mass."

"Agnes give ya a good whack with the rosaries?"

Alex asks if anyone's into going to Mass.

"Mass?" Peg says. "Mass?" That is the *last* place I'm goin. What's wrong with Howard Beach?"

The people in Howard Beach, Timmy explains to Joe, make life-size nativity scenes in their garages. Then they seal them in plastic, like enormous dioramas. Timmy also says there is no more midnight Mass at St. Francis. Then he asks Joe if he went to Catholic school.

"No way, man. My p's were hippies. They got home movies of me being born. Lotsa trippin people sittin around my living room."

"Cool." And even weirder than Ohio and tornadoes.

"Cool? They sent me to this communist school and named my sister Goldenrod."

"No."

"She changed it to Gloria last year."

"Gloria?" says Peg. "Weird. What do they do now?"

"Bowl."

All this is news to Alex. Why'd he tell these people he's just met? Maybe he made it up, for kicks—he's capable.

"I didn't know you had a sister."

"I still do."

"Why didn't you ever tell me?"

"You never asked."

Is that possible? "Neither did they."

"Whatsamatter?" says Timmy, sitting down and pulling his chair up close to Alex.

"What's the difference?" Joe mutters, and walks away toward the bar. The difference? She feels like something has popped inside her chest.

"You look tan," Timmy says. "Skiing?"

"Think it's dirt."

They take turns playing with the ashtray.

"I know," Timmy says. "We'll go shoot hoop. The *old* way." Alex pretends her shoe is untied so she can lean down and not have to look at him. Him and his remembering.

They used to shoot hoop a lot. Drunk. Barefoot. In the dark. You had to listen to know whether the ball even went in. Swish, the sound amplified in the empty schoolyard. Elaborate rules and penalties—when to play on one foot, with one hand, or backward, when to kiss, climb the fence, when to stop altogether and head for Timmy's showerhouse, where they would make out real quietly for fear of waking Mrs. Ray. They had to say everything in whispers, yes, exciting.

"Too cold for hoops," says Alex, thinking of the showerhouse, and of the extremely detailed crucifix Mrs. Ray had hanging there. Alex always covered it up, convinced it stared. But to Timmy, whose whole house was decked out in icons, one more piece of metal was nothing. Till once, in a reckless mood, he decided to remove the towel. Make instead a skirt, a little skirt on poor old Jesus. And that was the night they heard Mrs. Ray cry in her sleep. "Tiim-moothy." From the backyard they could hear it. "Tiim-moothy." Like her voice was bleeding. Of course, it was all a coincidence. Also a coincidence that Alex's bike had a flat, that some cats would pick *his* dead lawn to fight on.

"I remember hoops," Peg says.

Neither of them has the heart to say no, not those hoops. Particularly since they know she means CYO anyway. She and Alex played basketball for CYO all through school. Peg's father was their coach.

"And we were hot shit. Even though we weren't giants or nothin, we were hot."

"I guess so," Alex says, although Peg had always been the hot one. Alex was mostly average.

"You were OK for girls," teases Timmy, probably hoping he'll stir them up. But Peg's running off to call Chowder, and Alex, still all freaked out on memory, just sits there. Timmy's body was hard and gentle in the showerhouse. But still always a little too heavy for her.

"Let's leave." He's begging. "You and me."

"To?"

"Anywhere. Beach. Playground. Monkey bars, my—"

"It's wet out there."

"So."

"So it's wet out there."

Poor Timmy, big shoulders slumping, can see wetness for the bad excuse it is. He can see that it's no use trying to revive her old feeling. And where's Joe now? In the bathroom? Gone back to California in her car?

Peg has returned and is cracking up, pointing across the

bar. "See that guy, greasy hair, kickin in the cigarette machine? See him? You won't believe what he said to me."

Timmy smiles so his fucked-up bottom teeth show. "We believe anything. What?" But Peg has to finish laughing first.

" 'I've done thousands of dollars worth of cocaine, but my heart's never beat this fast.' He said that."

"Sounds like a song."

"A bumper sticker, 'I've done thousands of—' "

"I feel sick," says Joe, finally reappearing. He looks it too. To Alex, he's suddenly an intrusion.

"Figures," she says, like her mother, with her mouth closed. "It just figures."

Joe doesn't even ask what she means. "Could you gimme a fast massage? Right here?" He points to his pale, kind-of-blotchy neck. "Car rides always get me, ya know?" he continues to the table in general. An overly dramatic grimace. "Sittin in cars so long."

At school, Alex would have jumped up to do it. Now, she yawns. She's feeling almost at home.

Only what's wrong with Timmy? He's getting all red in the face, half-standing, and his hands slam down on the table.

"DO IT YOURSELF!" Display of anger that seems out of place but nice. It's what *she* should have said. "Don't order her around, and stop flicking ashes on my coat." A note of bitterness that tells Alex something. Tells her why those kids love that loud noise. It's simple. They can feel like they made it.

AT THE MOVIES | 8

Three-quarters through the double-feature matinee, *Planet of the Apes* and *Enter the Dragon*, the Park Theatre caught fire. Chowderhead's mom, in the third row, thought some kids were smoking pot, until Bruce Lee's face disappeared and she heard the alarm. One person died, a young boy, whom the firemen found only much later because he was so small that his head did not reach the top of the seat.

Chowderhead is doing push-ups when she bursts in. He has resorted to this, bored out of his mind by the golf tournament on "Wide World of Sports." TV sucks on Sundays; all the movies are in black and white. And winter sucks in Rockaway, with those same gray decisions over and over: TV or VCR, seven-card stud or anaconda sweat, vodka and orange or vodka and grapefruit.

Chowder likes working as a lifeguard in the summer. It means God as far as he's concerned. In winter, he hauls boxes at Mickey's Deli, which means Piece of Shit.

His mother sits in five different places in the room before she can get the story out. Chowder assumes she's won something—Publishers Clearing House or One-Hundredth Shopper. Nothing big. Nothing like what it is she finally tells him.

She hasn't been this excited, she says, since his brother Jim graduated bartender's school. And Chowder, well, he just can't believe it. A fire three blocks away, and he missed the whole fucking thing, watching that faggot game and grunting on the carpet. He had planned to go with her, too, even had his shoes on, till Timmy called. He could score a bag, he said. They'd drive down to Breezy Point and light up in the parking lot. It figures that Timmy never showed. Figures that Chowderhead missed the only exciting event in Rockaway since the drowned tally was announced in mid-September.

"If you woulda stepped outside," she says, "you woulda smelled the smoke," and she extends her arms out to illustrate—what? Big smoke? Then she settles down a little and sits on the couch in front of the TV and folds her long fingers in a knot. Chowder is sure she is not seeing or hearing about Crazy Eddie's Fourth of July Sale in February. She's seeing Bruce Lee: Bruce Lee melting up and feet racing down the red-carpeted slope towards the exit signs.

It must've been fun to use the special fire exit that you never got to use. And even more Chowder envied whoever it was that got to break the glass fire-alarm case with that little axe on a chain.

She's pleased with herself, that's clear. A man from Channel Nine even interviewed her. He'd picked her from all the people coughing in the snow out in front of the theater afterwards to interview. She'd be on the ten o'clock news.

"Lucky I put my face on this morning," she says. Who should she call, she wants to know, and "What do you think your father will have to say?"

She sounds as proud as a boy displaying scars. His father will not say a thing, Chowder thinks, but will only laugh, particularly if he sees her with that flat, happy face and still wearing the beaver coat. Half of Chowder wants to laugh too, only he can't. Even though she looks pretty funny, sitting there panting—what shabby fur. Even though in this state it'd be a cinch to get a few dollars off her. There is something else. That thing not said, underneath and only partly thought: She could be dead. The only mother in Rockaway who let her kids eat pizza for breakfast could be burned up dead.

He turns off the TV and asks if maybe she wants a drink or something to celebrate, because he does.

"I wish he'd get back," she says. "Wait till he hears."

"He" means Chowderhead's father, who's away a lot selling medical supplies to hospitals. In his absences Chowderhead's mother falls in love with Magnum P.I. or Kirk from that police show or, when she gets a chance, Bruce Lee.

"Bruce Lee is a nice man," she says in a way that bugs Chowder, as if he were the butcher or someone she knew personally.

"Bruce Lee's dead."

"He's too young to be dead."

"He is—right after *Enter the Dragon*, I remember."

"Couldn't be."

"It's true, right after *Enter the Dragon*, I'm telling you." She won't hear of it. Which is typical.

"Bruce Lee is a nice man," she keeps insisting. Chowder tells her nice people are boring and faggots. "Girls get turned off." She finds this extremely funny. Her eyes close and her laughs become snorts. Then she gets a bottle of wine for each of them from the kitchen, no glasses.

"That theater's been there since I was a girl," she says, like it's some important secret. "You'd get two newsreels and a double feature for fifty cents."

· · ·

Timmy comes in around eight-thirty without ringing the bell. There is not a single light on in the house. Chowder is practicing surfing moves on the coffee table for the benefit of his mother, who's asleep on the couch. He is glad to see Timmy until he remembers that it's Timmy's fault he missed the fire.

"Scumbag! Where've ya been?"

"Ya mean, ya didn't hear?"

"Of course I heard, asshole, she was there."

"Well, how do ya expect me to find any pot with everyone down at some fire?"

"*Me*, ya coulda found me," Chowder says, but doesn't really care, he's having too much fun. He yells, "Towering Inferno!" and falls on his mother's legs. She doesn't move.

"You're gonna wake her up."

"Burning, burning disco inferno," Chowder sings, even louder, just to annoy.

"You drunk?"

"You my mother?"

"You're sittin on her."

Chowder gets up off the couch. "She's a regular celebrity. Gonna be on the news." That shuts Timmy up. Chowder knows he's impressed even though it's pretty hard to impress Timmy, the nut.

"Really?"

"Let's get outta here," Chowder says. "I wanna see this thing."

"Burnt right in half. Half man, half woman."

"What the hell are you talkin about?"

"It's burnt in half."

"Well, let's see it."

"You gonna leave her here?"

"Yeah, why not, she's happy."

"In the dark and shit?"

"What else?"

"What if she doesn't wake up in time?"

Chowder gets a chill then, remembering that his mother could be dead. Lying there dead, not drunk. But he knows that that isn't what Timmy means. The news, she wouldn't want to miss the news. She'd die.

"VCR," Timmy says. "Tape it."

That's a good idea, and she'd never know he didn't think it up himself. Chowder walks over and sets up the machine, taping over "Magnum." Now she can show it to everyone who comes over. And she will too. Probably in slow motion and backwards also, just for kicks.

He lies down on the floor and thinks about this and then of his father, all wet from a shower maybe or half-asleep or arranging his medical supplies on the double bed in some motel. He'll flick on the TV for the hell of it, or maybe to see how the Jets are doing, and there she'll be on the TV, beaver coat and flat, happy face. What a riot. She'll be saying that "Bruce Lee was just doing his kicks and things like normal" when it happened.

And his father, Chowder tells Timmy, will be trying to order up vodka and something from room service but will be laughing too hard, his breasts jiggling, and have to hang up.

"Shut up," Timmy says, maybe because his own father is long gone. "You're gonna wake her."

Timmy is putting shoes on Chowder's feet. He hadn't even noticed.

"What am I, lame?"

"Yes," he says. "You are."

Chowder lets Timmy finish. It's easier. But he keeps on talking.

"I wish Mickey's would burn down. I should burn that hellhole down."

"Let's," says Timmy in a way that makes Chowder almost believe he means it.

He leaves a note on her stomach, on paper towels.

"Don't freak out," it says. "I taped it."

Outside feels good. They can hear music from Duffy's and other noise. Radios turned way up inside cruising cars, women yelling porch to porch, hordes of hysterical teenagers making snow forts. They point in the direction of the theater like enthusiastic tour guides. Everyone's smiling. It's as if the whole town has just come out of a coma, like Christmas. Better than Christmas, really: Christmas with none of the religious shit attached.

He wants to take off his coat. He wants to race. He wants to throw snowballs at the sides of houses.

Timmy walks slowly, says, "No one even knows how it started," and "The kid was in Sister Agnes's class."

"Better off dead."

Chowder can't tell whether Timmy laughs or just steps on something in the street.

Turning the corner, past the drugstore, then Woolworth's, then the beer distributor (once the public library), they are there. Timmy wasn't shitting. Half the theater perfectly normal and the other half gone. A pile of burnt things—fake velvet, wood, vinyl.

Still, it's not what he expected. Half man, half woman— that was a weird thing to say.

"Which half is which?"

"What?"

"Before, you said half man, half woman. Which half are we?"

"I didn't think of that," Timmy says.

"You said it."

"I know, but I didn't think of that."

"We're the burnt half, I guess," Chowder says, trying to balance himself on the icy curb. "Did the kid like burn up or breathe smoke, whatever it's called?"

"Smoke inhalation."

"That's all?"

"No, that's what it's called."

"Well, what then?"

"What?"

"Is the kid toast?"

"Shut up, man."

"Well?"

"I think a little of both. A little burnt, a little outta breath."

Neither of them says anything for a while after that. Timmy glares without turning his head. Like he's been thinking of something and he's been disturbed. This happens a lot. Chowder can never figure out what the hell Timmy has to think about all the time when they do exactly the same things. Maybe he's thinking about the dead kid. But Alex would be a safer bet.

"Who was he?" Chowder asks.

"Who?"

"The kid."

"One of the Murphys, 'cept he was twelve or something, not really a kid, just short."

"Oh."

They turn and head towards Duffy's, across the street, and it's odd because they turn and walk over at precisely the same time, without saying anything. Does Timmy notice?

Inside is dark. Decorations left over from Christmas, though it's already February. Rudolph, Santa, and a string of colored lights. They're sort of torn up and falling down, and only five of the lights work, all yellow for some reason.

At Duffy's a microphone gets passed around. Old men sing "When Irish Eyes Are Smiling" and "Yankee Doodle Dandy," talk about their wives, fishing tackle, war (any), and who is missing that night. When some old guy is missing from Duffy's, no one knows whether he'll be gone for good or if he just isn't feeling well.

It's a howl of a place and all, but you wouldn't take a girl there. The place smells of hair tonic, piss. Mostly they go on Sundays, when Louie the Lump is bartending.

Chowder gets a table by the window so they can look out at the theater. It surprises him that the table isn't already taken, though there is one guy nearby, fat and sleeping with his head dropped onto his chest.

Everyone is talking about the fire. "Murphy's got enough kids," and "Hope some of them roaches in there got burnt." Some of them bragging about how they were around before the theater was even built, saw the first show. But nobody can remember what it was.

Looking closer, Chowder sees that the guy asleep has his false teeth between his legs on the chair, right at the edge. Maybe they fell out. It would be nice of me, Chowder thinks, to slide them further onto the chair in case someone bangs into him. They might fall on the floor.

But he can't do it, doesn't want to touch them. They're yellow. They remind him of the sample teeth in the glass case at the dentist's, of the glow-in-the-dark vampire fangs he wore every Halloween for seven, eight years, of dead people in movies who can only be identified by their fillings. Running his tongue along his teeth, he squints out the window and thinks he sees someone moving around by the theater. Little Murphy's ghost or a cat or something.

"Almost time for Mom," Timmy says and hands Chowder a Black Russian. It is, they have decided, the appropriate drink.

"Look at this guy," Chowder says, pointing to the false teeth. "Jesus."

"Drink up," says Timmy.

"Aren't false teeth supposed to be white?"

"Maybe he smokes with 'em in."

"Or it's the yellow light."

"Yeah."

"Why'd we come in here?" Chowder says.

"I don't know."

"What'd Louie have to say?"

"About what?"

"Anything."

"Nothing."

Mr. Cox is on the microphone telling his usual story about how he used to be a Hollywood producer, a millionaire and everything, until he found Jesus and gave all his money away. Timmy never believes him since he's always bumming, but Chowder believes because some nights the old man will sink two hundred bucks into the Joker Poker machine without flinching. Now that's balls, that's millionaire mentality.

But Timmy can't stand the guy. One night he made Cox swim on his stomach from one end of the bar to the other before he'd give him a dollar thirty-five for cigarettes. Cox did it, too. Chowder figures it's the Jesus stuff that pisses Timmy off. He's weird about Jesus; whether it's because he believes or doesn't believe, Chowder isn't sure.

Timmy gets up and puts money in the jukebox. Nothing in there that either of them would want to hear. To shut Cox up is obviously the idea. No one protests. No one could care. They've all heard his story before. But Cox starts singing along to the jukebox playing "New York, New York" and soon everyone is singing. Even Louie the Lump is pounding on the cash register. Everything is OK.

Then Timmy returns to the table looking mad. He's shouting.

"What's everyone so fuckin happy about?"

"You know."

"All the old men who never outgrew Death Kegs." When a lifeguard loses a swimmer he has to buy a keg and everyone is allowed to abuse him the entire evening.

The fat man wakes up and bolts his head around as if he's scared, as if he doesn't know where he is. Chowder feels sorry for him and tries to smile and points at the teeth on the chair. He can't understand what the guy is saying. He points to the teeth again and the man nods, slips them in his mouth. Still, Chowder can't make out the words. Either the man is forgetting to move his mouth to form them or else Chowder is too drunk to hear.

Because Timmy seems to be hearing fine. He's telling the fat man to go home and sleep. Describing how comfortable his bed will be. How does Timmy know the man's bed is comfortable, or if he has a bed at all?

Timmy's just being nice. Bruce Lee is a nice man. Timmy is a nice man. Nicer to strangers than to people he knows. Mean to Cox. Nice to fat man. Both to Chowder. Timmy is a nut.

The clock over the bar says ten. Louie has disappeared into the freezer, probably to smoke a joint without them, so Chowder goes over and unplugs the jukebox himself. No one stops singing. "These vagabond shoes / Are longing to stray." Then he picks up the microphone.

"Channel Nine!" he yells. "The fire!"

It works. They all freeze, look at him, waiting. His face feels hot.

"TV" he says. "It's gonna be on TV."

So the TV finally gets turned on and everyone is silent like they're in church or something, all standing there in front of the Sony, worshiping a commercial for Hanes underwear. An androgynous-looking woman punches at a pair of men's briefs, apparently to test them, and a little girl says, "When I grow up, I want to be just like you . . . a fussbucket."

Timmy is the only one laughing. The rest of the bar is funeral-quiet, even Chowder, who finds the word "fuss-bucket" very peculiar and Timmy's laugh a little out of control.

More commercials. Jovan Musk, helping American men stay sexy. Then one for steel-belted radial tires. It's like waiting for the ball to drop in Times Square, everyone drunk and standing around ready to kiss each other and jump up and down.

"We're gonna be on the map," Timmy whispers, flicking his swizzle stick. Chowder visualizes the peninsula as it looks on the map of New York in his basement. Rockaway, just a tiny strip that hangs off Queens as if it isn't sure whether it wants to break away and become an island or hang on tighter, desperate not to be abandoned. Yeah, it's already on the map, but you could easily cover it up with one dumb little swizzle stick.

When the news comes on they all cheer, then listen eagerly. A mugging. A chain of disgusting nursing homes. A suicide, and Reagan's vacation in Santa Barbara. Chowder hates Reagan for being in Santa Barbara, where it's warm. The guy doesn't even surf, what a waste. The news says he likes to ride around on horses. Probably also golfs, the fag. Maybe Nancy lusted after Bruce Lee the way his mother did, while Ron went around the world or cursed out Russia on the phone. But Nancy was never in a fire and *his* mother was.

It is already twenty after. He wonders what happened to his other friends—Bean, Lefty, Artie, Peg—but he doesn't really care. Timmy is here. Timmy put on his shoes for him. Maybe he and Timmy really would burn Mickey's down, and then drive away to Santa Barbara and never return.

When it finally comes on, Chowder's stomach is making weird noises. The newscaster's face doesn't move. It's all the same to him. While he tells about the fire, a small picture flashes on the screen behind his head. A graphic symbol of flames with the word "Fire" written in wavy letters, diagonally across. It looks like a street sign.

The footage of the theater is short and the fire already over. They show the kid being taken out in a blanket and then Chowder's mom saying "The exit was orderly." You can tell she said more but they cut it. That's all.

Timmy slaps Chowder on the back and the whole bar makes noise, congratulating themselves. Only Timmy knows it was Chowder's mother on TV. Louie, who would've recognized her, is still doing a doobie in the freezer or talking on the phone to his girlfriend. The man with the false teeth missed the whole thing, sleeping again. Cox is now running around shaking people's hands and saying, "Jesus loves you."

"Let's go," says Timmy. "My brain hurts."

"It'll have to come out."

"Let's torch it."

"Your brain?"

"No, Mickey's."

They stand outside. It's too early to go home and Chowder doesn't want to go to another bar. They'll tease him about his mother saying "The exit was orderly." What kind of thing is that to say? Why doesn't she care about the dead kid? Why doesn't he? Timmy does, you can tell.

Chowder is confused, in a way panicked, all of a sudden. On TV his mother's hair, blown by the wind, hovered above her head like a spirit. He wishes he had gloves.

"We're goin to the movies," Timmy says and starts walking across the street. His voice sounds as if he might be holding in a laugh, but he is not smiling. Chowder follows.

The snow is spotted black in places and packed down hard, perfect for skitching if there were any cars. They enter the theater as they normally would, because that's the part that is still intact. Timmy even pretends to pay an invisible person for a ticket and holds his hand out in the lobby for someone to tear it.

"I keep the stubs," he says. "Memorabilia."

Chowder's mom keeps her stubs in a shoebox under the sink. Does Timmy know that? The air inside is thick, warm, makes him dizzy. Timmy says it smells like that time when a candle tipped over in church and burned the carpet.

Timmy was an altar boy up until the fifth grade, when a nun hit him over the head with his own Star Trek lunchbox and he hit back. A left hook to Sister Annunciata in the jaw. If Chowder had done it he would've gotten expelled, but Timmy was only suspended because Sister Agnes is his aunt. That's OK, though. Chowder got to see it. The whole class got to see. It was like Timmy was defending them all. Like Bruce Lee. They would have cheered if they hadn't been so terrified.

Timmy's funny that way. He'll go knock out a nun, but then he won't fight a geek like that guy Alex brought home for Christmas. Chowder starts to make fun of Timmy for writing all those love letters. Like he's the first person ever to get dumped. And for his ant farm, and for hardly ever washing his hair.

But just then he hears a noise. And not his stomach. Something alive. The familiar squeaking of a wheelchair is amplified in the big lobby.

"*Holy shit*, it's Seaver, Seaver's in here." And sure enough, Seaver wheels himself partially out of a shadow and nods once like he's been expecting them. The red hair on his arms glimmers when a car drives past the theater.

They call him Seaver for that amazing arm. For the way he sits on corners in his rusty old chair, nailing cars with snowballs. And people say he was once with the Mets—although Timmy, of course, doesn't believe a word of it. "The Mets aren't *that* old." But who knows how old Seaver is?

Chowderhead hasn't seen him since last week at Mickey's. Behind Mickey's Seaver's got a whole shitload of Salvation Army clothing and a mattress with an umbrella poked through it. Chowder sneaks him beer or salami from the store and goes to eat his own lunch back there most days. You can say anything to Seaver; he's cool. Chowder swears he can understand Seaver's talk, too. They're both redheads, after all. When Chowder's mouth is full they sound almost identical. He's sure the bum got his tongue cut out as a prisoner of some war.

Seaver waves to them from behind the candy counter. He is stuffing his face full of melted Snickers, M&Ms, malted milk balls, and very burnt popcorn.

"Paradise," Timmy says. "He's in heaven."

He rolls Seaver away from the counter, but the bum stretches out his hands to say he's not finished.

"You'll get sick," Timmy says and pushes him down the red-carpeted slope. Then he runs past to catch him at the other end.

"He's gonna puke if you do that," Chowder says, feeling sick himself.

But Timmy only shakes his head, pelts Chowder with a handful of Good & Plenty.

"Can't you see?" he says. Like there isn't any question. *"He's in heaven."*

HAT WALK | 9

It's tough taking someone seriously who's wearing a shower cap, but Peg demands attention. Fun's hard work. Walking down Rockaway's mile strip of bars in a hat and stopping to drink in every one (old men bars, kiddie bars included), that's hard work. And with half a mile still to go, and though it might conceivably take all night, Peg's determined. Says rules are rules. The custom, a must. A DIFFERENT DRINK AT EACH, as if to ensure sickness.

Already Timmy has lost a glove, who knows where. A million possible spaces for a glove between there and here. Could've disguised itself as a clump of sawdust in Park Tavern or stuck in midair after some gesture he'd made. One glove, so dumb, as useless as one shoe. Nothing left to do but throw it out.

But it's cold. An added hardship. Colder than a witch's zit, or whatever that expression is. A deep freeze, Peg says, news says it's record-breaking, "like sub-existable."

An incredible temperature for the first days of March. She's claiming that earlier today her just-washed hair froze when she took out the garbage. And with schools closed, the kids played duel with giant icicles, or hockey on puddles, or Eskimo with bushes for igloos.

Peg's all worked up, voice squeaky, almost gone. She's breathing hard between swallows of gin and ginger ale, pushing Chowder's head off her lap. Meaning that she is not happy. Something is very wrong.

It's like this. She'd gone out psyched to join the ice games, *running* to join, but some kid said, "Let the lady pass," and they scattered. Flash, they all disappeared. LADY? How unbelievably weird. You have no idea how it felt. Might as well kill herself before it gets worse. She'll have cellulite in no time. She'll be carrying stale coffee candies in a purse. LADY? Oh God, how did that happen?

Chowder laughs. The pom-poms bounce on his dumb green Jets hat.

"No, biggie. We know you ain't a lady." He tries again for her thigh.

"Lay off," Timmy warns, unable to recall ever seeing Peg this upset, except once, in pain, at the Lifeguard Olympics, when that small animal Sloane fell on top of her with a respirator.

Now her eyes are everywhere, as if she'd never seen the interior grim of Roger's Irish House, but they're also nowhere, as if she isn't even seeing it now. All because some kids split on her? It makes no sense. And doesn't Chowder notice? How can he be trying to hit on her tonight? And leaving Timmy to come to her defense? Well, they were just getting wasted, he guessed. And sure, he'd stay by her, think up something, or try, and he'd do it out of something more than concern for Peg. He's been hooked in by the mention of Alex.

Peg said she called Alex in New Hampshire, where Timmy pictures it being nine times as cold. Pictures Alex all alone in this little phone booth, quivering. Oh.

But it's time to go, and since everyone's been too cold to dare remove their coats, they're ready. Bean first in the cardboard McDonald's hat he wears working the drive-thru, followed by a parade of all the headgear you could dream up—baseball caps, painter's caps, icebags, snap tweed and hunter's caps, chef's, cowboy's, sailor's hats, football helmets and visors, berets and hoods, wigs, an Indian headdress, a fez, a lamp shade, an aluminum pot. Artie's got on his father's police outfit. Louie the Lump, his grandmother's plastic rain bonnet. And Timmy wears the propeller beanie that he sent away for in fourth grade, along with sea monkeys and magic rocks. Obsessive even then, he had saved, saved those Lucky Charms box tops. It was the one sugar cereal his mother allowed, Timmy thought now, because the leprechaun on the label made it vaguely Irish.

He wonders if it'd cheer Peg up to show her what else was in the closet where he found the beanie. Torso of G.I. Joe, stack of very yellow *Archies*, a cap gun, some Matchbox cars, and a note she herself once wrote, asking—did he like Alex? Imagine.

The members of the hat parade take full advantage of their big boots, a stomping exit, heads high and rolling. Outside waits the already loyal mutt Chowder found in a doorway three bars back. So black, the animal looks purple. A shivering mess of hair, bones, tongue that Peg bends down to hug. *She* needs a hug, Timmy thinks, but she might get the wrong idea or he might get the wrong idea or Chowder might. The hugs, they're Chowder's department anyhow, so Timmy walks close beside her instead.

Peg says that when her father's car skidded slow-motion into the garage door, she decided her dirty laundry could wait. She just *had* to go out and play, and if she was too big for those stupid kids, well, why not the hat walk? Last year she said she'd never do it again, but, then, that was last year.

Only, too bad it's too cold for snow. They could've built forts. With this many people, they could've had a full-fledged snowball war. Everyone against Sloane.

Timmy watches Peg watch Chowder watch the dog. The dog is without any traction on the ice, scrambles helplessly. Hilarious. The dog becomes the cause of much running and sliding, and of course it is Peg who eventually glides by them all, perfectly straight line. With this amazingly graceful swoop she turns just in time, at the door to Duffy's.

Inside she heads for the jukebox. The old men give the troops a round of applause, remembering their own hat days or pretending to. Stories of who did what that time. The kind of gibberish that makes Timmy sick, sad, afraid. If he lay down now he could fall asleep like Rip Van, wake up a drunk, smelly old guy without socks. Oh Rotaway, the place Alex used to call home and maybe still did, to get a laugh in New Hampshire.

"If I Said You Have a Beautiful Body Would You Hold It Against Me" is the song Peg picks. She's staring out the window at the burnt-down movie theater rumored to become a roller rink. She's taking the drink Chowder gives her and gulping at it without even looking to see what it is. Then, not liking whatever it is that Chowder whispers in her ear, she snaps back (Timmy can't hear what) and walks off with the drink toward the bathroom.

"What *is* her problem?" Chowder asks Timmy by the bar. "I didn't do shit."

"That's true."

"I don't think she likes me anymore. Maybe she likes you."

"Don't be an asshole."

"Maybe she's on the rag."

"You're bein an asshole."

"I didn't do shit."

"Sometimes," says Timmy, "you're just deaf to the world."

But Chowder's distracted by Sloane's balancing-on-a-swivel-stool act and he doesn't answer. Sloane is standing on one leg, his head nearly touching the ceiling. His body is huge, messy, but he manages not to fall and he gives up only when the chair breaks.

The by now rather large audience goes on watching, waiting for the next feat. They don't mind Sloane's poor excuse for a hat, just a stocking with one hole poked through—not for breathing, for drinking. They don't mind how hideous his already hideous features look, covered by stocking. No, Sloane's appeal to the group, to a drunk group, is remarkable. Fitzy, the greenish bartender in a parka, knows it, and a look on his face says he won't dare test it. After all, one broken stool is a helluva lot better than a whole trashed bar. No need to make enemies, now, is there? No prob, thing was ancient, don't you give it another thought.

Timmy examines the damage. The stool will never be repaired. It will be there from now on, a trophy with its story attached—what a crazy guy that Sloane is, or, from the bonehead himself, the night I broke this very stool.

His crew listens intently. Another of Sloane's genius theories. How for every white man there's an identical black. They are actually taking him seriously, nodding like, oh yeah, so true. Sloane's own black double naturally being no less than Muhammad Ali. Timmy could see himself standing there saying crap like that. No one would so much as look up. Timmy could scream, tear off his hat, and fall down, and probably no one would even notice. It's something he's realizing slowly. The key to being big is just being big.

Though the crowd had considerably dwindled since Danny's, since Sullivan's, The Breakers, Emerald Isle, there are also a few new recruits. Uptown guys, all Steves or Daves, in ski jackets. They're quiet, clean-cut, but seem cool enough. Ready to put shirts on their heads in the correct spirit.

Uncle John's has a live show. Sam Roach, "THE KING OF BLARNEY. THE BOB HOPE OF IRELAND." He's a slimy guy, big freckled ears and orange polyester, but his voice is fine, deep, mentholated. Timmy's convinced he's lip-synching.

"Should be bald" is Peg's appraisal. "He gives the impression of baldness, ya know?"

"No, I don't know," Chowder says. "He ain't even receding in the hairline."

And Timmy agrees, she's out of her mind. Blarney King has got a big white pompadour.

"He just *seems* like the bald type is all." She practically falls down trying to stand. "Getting up too quick is like tin foil," she says, and she grabs the table with both hands to steady herself. Whoa, Timmy thinks, this girl is blicked. While Chowderhead goes into hysterics.

Maybe he understands about the foil or maybe he just feels like laughing. But whatever it is, his face flushes and he bends over, clutching the chair, shaking his hat off. His hair glints like copper shavings.

Timmy and Peg look at each other and that's it. A collective laughing fit, although none of them knows what's funny. They're laughing at each other laughing, and that's funny, and when it starts getting bad and they're gasping, "My stomach hurts," "I'm gonna pee in my pants," slowly other people giggle in bits, and then it's continuous, growing. More people and more. Timmy, for some reason, can think only of poor King Blarney and how he must be sure they're all laughing at him. And that's really funny. Makes him laugh even harder.

Sloane, who's possibly the only one not cracking up, seizes the opportunity to yell "BELLYSLIDE!" and to grab people's drinks. One by one, he pours them all out on the floor. "BEL-

LYSLIDE!" The bartender tries to give him shit but is laughing. All alone, with no one helping, Sloane manages to create a little river of alcohol for himself. Then he strips. Of course leaving the stocking hat on, but he strips, he's standing there in like zero degrees without anything on. Everyone clams up. Maybe shock. His flock becomes attentive again.

Ignoring the bartender, who can't seem to do much anyhow, Sloane backs up as far as he can, all the way back till he's leaning on the women's bathroom door. Then, with a running start he's off and diving flat on the floor. A real professional, from all the practice he's had jumping off jetties. His slide is exquisite, and he's having a ball. Howls all the way across. Applause when he bangs his head on the wall at the other end. Some of his friends start chanting, "SLOANE, SLOANE, SLOANE," and the boys with shirts on their heads (new fans) circle around him, still clapping.

Timmy's amused mostly because Blarney King goes on singing through it all, as if none of it were even happening. Peg wants to do it herself sometime, only not in a bar, and Chowderhead complains that he smells dog shit.

Yeah, things are beginning to cook. Seaver even risks the ice to wheel out of the burnt-down theater (his new home until it becomes a roller rink) and wave as they approach. He especially likes the dog, wants to keep it. He's given coins, lots, by the hat walkers, all generous from drink. But they're not thinking about him really. Only Chowder, Timmy, Peg stay behind, intent on finding food. What good will money do the guy with everything except bars closed? There's one alternative. To break into the place where the boys work. Mickey's Deli.

As is expected, Peg takes no persuading. She should have thought of it herself, she says. "Yea, Robin Hood!" She walks around in circles on her hands. She makes a list of what they'll need. Tries to carve in ice with a shell bit she just *happens* to have in her pocket. Timmy can't stop himself from kissing her. Right on the forehead where the shower cap ends. Surprise—it isn't cold but burning. And surprise—Chowderhead does not appear to mind.

"Oranges, salami, something crunchy, and a lottery ticket" is what she comes up with.

"A lottery ticket?" Chowder whisper-laughs, as he pries open the window in back. The storeroom window that he and Timmy always leave unlocked.

"Imagine Seaver winning the lottery!" Peg shrieks. "Imagine he gets billions of dollars and buys a yacht and takes us on vacation permanently." Then, apparently a new thought, "Let's rearrange all the food on the shelves!"

By which time they are already inside and not knowing quite how to proceed. Peg must be calmed. She wants to do all kinds of ridiculous things, like turn on the radio and make coffee. She insists Seaver needs protein and they should open the plastic vat of chicken salad.

All her suggestions are vetoed.

"The idea is speed," Timmy says, "speed and deftness."

"Deafness? Why deafness?"

"Forget it. Let's just do this thing."

But Chowderhead's leading her around like it's his house or something. Bragging how in the storeroom you'd survive a nuclear war. He knows what Peg likes, shows her where everything's kept, then sets them up an obstacle course— around the bleach, over the tuna, like that. There are rats. They patter on the concrete floor and make Timmy paranoid. There's also a smell, hard to place—produce, Lysol— making him nauseated. But Chowder and Peg won't quit fucking around, now they're racing on dollies. Timmy decides to collect stuff himself, careful that each item is from an already open supply. Bread, cake, bananas, and a jar of peanut butter.

"Too bad they don't sell coats," Peg says as they walk back to the movie theater. She's clearly disappointed in the escapade. Too serious. Too short. Reverting to her earlier mope, she chews on her mitten ends, says it's a joke—peanut butter and no knife. And think of all the fun Alex must be having in the country. Seaver's not worried about silverware, though, and Peg knows that. More than pleased with the gift, he winks, hugs their legs together, a true sweep of thanks.

He's all set up there in the theater lobby. A refrigerator-sized cardboard box that he found just this week. Has a hobby even, points proudly to the row of tin cans he's polished to the gleam point. He does not want to come along, wants the dog. But the dog won't stay, faithfully follows Chowderhead away to the Blackwater Inn.

The Blackwater's packed with high-school girls who've somehow convinced their parents that it's the Ice Age. Geometry's obsolete. They've been let out on the protest that they'll be just down the street. They've met at the house of the one girl whose parents overtrust or just don't give a shit.

Peg lets Chowder and Timmy in on this bit of young women's world like she's doing a service, but Chowder's not listening, only watching her lips move. Nice lips, littlish, smooth, and sucking a single beer nut.

The rest of the nuts go to the dog, who's been taught to retrieve, says Chowder, "by some distant owner"; says Peg, "in another life"; says Timmy, "by instinct." In any case, three bags of nuts have already been flung around the room.

Chowderhead crouches by Peg's chair, mouth open for a nut, but he doesn't get one. She's ignoring him. He tries to stand. Vision blackens. A bad rush. He'll just stay on the floor. Safer. Rest. A new view to accompany Peg's ongoing nostalgia soundtrack. What crap it is anyhow. How can she say she misses high school? She hated high school. How can she say she liked lying to her parents, always fighting with her parents and running away? She misses Alex.

It was Alex's house where she'd stay. The little basement room with its own entrance. They could come in at five, six o'clock. They could smoke pot and pretend they were in a bomb shelter.

Under the table Chowder can see Timmy's leg muscles tense. The very utterance "Alex" and he's off having convulsions. It's sick, no offense to Alex, *it just isn't normal.*

"Oh, how is she?" (By the way.)

Chowder knows Timmy cannot resist.

"What did she have to say on the phone? Anything to me? Is she coming home soon? Is she having fun? I mean, is she seeing anyone?"

Chowderhead's almost embarrassed for him. Guy's got no pride. If he did he'd understand lots of things better. Why Alex is sick of him, for one. For another, why Chowder's not about to mother Peg. So she's too old for ring-around-the-rosy. *So what?*

And now that Timmy has found out that Alex only said hi on the phone, not I love you madly forever but just hi, he joins Peg in her funk. Nothing worse than a guy who pouts, except maybe a pouty girl paying more attention to the dog than to you. The two of them together are just one big explosion of gloom. Straining his neck up from the floor, Chowder makes the two fixed frowns into four, six, then loses interest.

Laughing doesn't catch this time. Chowder calls the dog, who won't come. Retrievehead's got some new friends. The Steves and Daves have taken over the game, throwing

M&Ms. Chowder is sure they have cocaine because they're sniffing a lot, going to the bathroom in groups a lot, and not offering him any. Since he can't follow their conversation—politics, colleges, skiing—they bug him. He decides he does not like their boots. And that traitor mutt, he decides, is not getting a name.

Everyone's an idiot, but at least Sloane knows how to have fun. The only reason their rugby team, the Fishheads, ever wins is Sloane, inciting the scrum. "Get animal!" he'll scream when they're just about to run. Or "Fearless, fearless, Guinness for breakfast." Here Sloane has found another activity. Chowder locates his big legs across the room. They're wrapped around other legs, almost as big, in jeans with useless little ankle zippers, ending in high beige pumps.

Chowder should just dump Peg, she's hardly a girlfriend. Find himself a nice fifteen-year-old of his own. He's not so keen on being grown-up either.

"Lose something?" Lefty asks, bending down so fast that his yarmulke lands on Chowder's shoulders.

"Yeah, my dinner. Lost that a couple of hours ago." Chowder says, happy with his joke, happy someone is noticing him. He pockets the yarmulke for the next time his mother needs cheering. He'll just appear one day with this thing on his head. Hee. Hee.

"Whataya doin on the floor?" Lefty wants to know and lies down as well.

"Oh, I see now . . . this is good . . . yeah . . . *much* better. You feel, you feel like—"

"Like ya can't fall."

Lefty sort of groans as the hand holding his drink becomes limp. He's asleep. He's snoring. Brandy seeps into his hair. Chowder isn't sure whether to leave him there or to carry him along to the next, (thank God) last bar.

. . .

It's hot, cold, hot, nothing, numb. Timmy puts his one glove in the mailbox. Lots of shouting—something under ice. On the ice, Sloane's new woman, wobbly-cautious in her high beige pumps. Dog barking like a drill through your head. Dog barking, barking—seagull carcass somehow frozen whole and now part of the street. A lump in the street.

They circle around and kick at it. Eye open and a broken wing. Poor thing, they all think in unison, except Peg. To her, a bird corpse isn't interesting; the dog is. "The animal who smells through ice!"

How nice to see her smile, her face nuzzle the matted fur. Removing her shower cap, Peg makes a short, nonsensical speech, then crowns the beast.

"AAAAAALEX!"—under the pool table, scrounging for a ball?! Timmy is all shook up when who stands up instead but Alicia McHenry. What is he, insane? Thinking Alicia McHenry from Mickey's Deli was Alex?

"Mr. Timmy Ray!" she says in a way that at least assures him he yelled Alex's name only in his mind.

"You OK? Sit. Ya made it, hurrah! Was it fun? Didya puke? Are ya broke yet?"

Oh shut up. You're not Alex, you're not even close. You wear the most makeup of any girl alive and use words like hurrah. You'll be working in that hellhole deli till the day you die or till they make you manager and I never could stand your voice, thinks Timmy, walking away.

He's determined to have his last drink since he's gotten this far, but it's hard keeping the room from whirling and his too-small propeller beanie is starting to make his brain vibrate.

"You hate me, don't you?" asks Alicia, following. "You're

all red. You never talk to me at work no more. Where's Chowderhead? Cute hat. Can I maybe borrow five dollars?"

Where *is* Chowder, he wonders, jerking around to look. But sees—Alex. In that fraction of a second his head takes to pass Alicia's face, he sees something of Alex. Of course it's only a little near the mouth, if you glimpse fast, drunk, but what the hell. He'll loan her the five bucks just for that.

Aware of his stare, Alicia licks her lips. Frosty gluelike gloss, really horrifying. What's *really* horrifying—he had sex with her once at a Death Keg and remembers not remembering it till she told him the next day.

To act regular, he begins the story about breaking into Mickey's, but he feels so fuzzy, so distant, and then Peg is there asking where Chowder is. "Did he say he was pointing Lefty home? No one's seen him since the frozen seagull." Her voice seems to get further and further away, ends up sounding behind glass.

"Please, let's go."

Alicia asking, "Who, me?" all giggly.

"Sorry, no," Peg tells her and leads Timmy out.

He's looking for good cold air, a bed, and, oh yeah, Chowderhead. But right away it's the dog, a different sort of bark this time, a growl-whine coming from the schoolyard across the street. And running, well, Peg's running, he's run-walking behind, they hear other noises, ice crunching and voices. McGlackity! Glack, Glack, McGlackity! Then, Hebe. Fuckin Hebe. Mick. Hebe. Do it again. C'mon, hit me, you fuckin Jew boy. Mick scum. C'mon, hit me!

And getting closer, the motions of two figures in the dark. So near one another in the dark they could be mistaken for lovers if you didn't hear Dirty McGlackity, Mama's boy, Jew boy, breathing at each other those same two, three insults. Over and over and over.

The fight has reached the shoulder-pushing stage. Chowder and one of the Shirtheads, Steve or Dave. They make circles with their arms like messy breaststrokes.

"HELP ME OUT!" is Chowder's yell-whisper when he sees them. "Timmy, man, help me out. We'll fuck him up good. Let's fuck him up!" Timmy stands there not knowing what to do, the plea turns plead, "TIMMMMEEE, HELP!" and to Peg, "Do something, asshole!" So he grabs Chowder, pulls him back, struggles to keep him back during a fresh assault. Dirtbag mick McGlack.

Chowder, unable to pull out of Timmy's grip, still manages to get one hand free. Remembers about Lefty's yarmulke sitting in his pocket.

"Want your beanie, Jew boy?! Want your diaphragm?!" He spits. Direct hit. And Shirthead really loses it, lunging quick but intercepted by Peg, who beats on him like a man but isn't one and so doesn't get hit back, gets thrown on the ice instead.

"You gotta sic your woman on me?! You gotta sic your white-trash woman on me?! You chickenshit mick motherfucker." He screams himself out of the schoolyard and disappears long before his curses do.

You would have sworn something burst then. The three of them all beginning to shout at once. No one stopping to listen, each lost in a private fit. Peg, "I'm no one's fucking woman! I ripped my pants, shit!" Chowder, let loose and kicking the fence, "Some friend you are, he hits me with a bottle and gets away with it?! Friends fight for each other, not like you, you *coward*!" And Timmy, "Friends? Friends stop fights, jerk, and two on one just isn't cool."

Chowder turns to march out of the schoolyard and Timmy sees the blood. Face all blood.

"You all right?" Too late.

"See what ya did now?" says Peg, picking up the dog and

following. The dog somehow still has the shower cap on, is howling sad now, goes away. They've all gone away without him, back into the bar.

Timmy leans on the fence and swallows hard. Eyes closed feel on fire. A different dog crying in the distance? In his head? Trying to speak but only a bark comes out. What would it say? He was right—peace, man. He was wrong—chickenshit mick motherfucker. Would Alex have gone with Chowder and Peg anyway? Would Alex . . . Should he say he's sorry? *Is* he sorry? Is it already tomorrow or just ice being bright? Squeezing the cold rust of fence, an attempt at what? To hold on to something. But there's nothing, nothing, a schoolyard full, a hole he bites on the inside of his cheek. Then, a sudden voice. Deep. ANOTHER SHIRTHEAD.

"Hey, where'd your friend go? Where is he? He hit my brother. Where is he? I'm gonna slaughter that motherfucker, I'm gonna—"

But Timmy's sprung, body on body on the ground. He's pounding, can't stop himself, pounding, pounding, pounding, all around that bark-cry that's not real, and not feeling anything. Dark hair on ice. Flesh on ice. Fist in flesh like nothingness, pounding an anonymous face, so—good. I hate you all. I hate this place.

10 | MOVING MATTERS

Alex isn't sure how long Peg's been there but she looks giant, standing over the bed, a six of Molson's, open bag of barbecue chips, and a map.

"You're gonna haveta show me how to get here," is all she says when Alex's eyes open.

"But you're here."

"No, baby, you're in Rockaway."

"Rockaway? . . . What? . . . Oh."

"Gullible as ever."

"What?"

Alex pulls back the covers. Fuzzy spots like someone has just taken her picture and she sees the sheets are striped yellow in places where a highlighter has leaked.

"What are you doing here?"

"What are you doing in bed at four in the afternoon?"

"I fell asleep dreaming, I mean reading. You wouldn't believe the weird shit I was dreaming."

"Like I was here?" Peg sits straddling Alex, her face up real close. "I *do* only exist in your dream, you know," poking the ticklish place not many people know about, near Alex's hipbone.

"Stop screwin with my brain, please," says Alex, swinging at Peg with the pillow. "What the hell are you doing here?"

"Thought I'd drop by and watch you sleep."

"You don't *drop by* New Hampshire."

"OK!" Peg pins Alex's arms down. "I'm sick of hearin how cool you are, up at this place for free and shit. I'm just seein what the big deal is."

"Who says it's a big deal?"

"Ya know . . . everyone."

"Yeah, I know. Timmy. Now Timmy's everyone?"

When she says "Timmy," Peg's grip tightens, then gets even tighter the second time.

"I'm just makin sure college girl isn't gettin too smart on us, *see?*"

"Sure, but quit calling me that—Miss Hawaiian."

It's the only equivalent name she can think of. Surprisingly, Peg seems to like it. Alex can feel the hands on her wrists slowly releasing, asks, "You got Chowderhead and Louie the Lump hiding in your car or what?"

"No."

"You miss me?"

"No." She moves away and sits on the floor. "I've missed seeing you."

Alex finds the highlighter under the covers. Also a book, *Coming of Age in Samoa,* a small pair of nail scissors, not hers, and a sock whose match is still on her foot. She examines the scissors for a minute, trying to figure out how they got there, then throws all the stuff on the floor.

"Quite a collection," Peg says. "What's in *there?*" pointing to the other bed, where Roommate and Lars are asleep. Alex hadn't even noticed.

"That what you all do here? Sleep?"

"It's midterm." Alex says, "Didntcha have midterm at Kingsborough?"

"I dropped out before midterm."

"Why?"

"Timmy must've told you about the fire extinguishers."

"So."

"Also my psych teacher was a Nazi."

"So."

"It sucked."

Alex gives up. When Peg doesn't feel like answering a question, she won't, that's it. But also, maybe that was it. It sucked. Wasn't that Timmy's whole reason for dropping out of high school?

"So how's everything in Malibu Queens?"

"Same. They're buildin a new parkin lot."

"I meant you. How are you?"

"Oh, just elegant," Peg says.

"Elegant" was one of those bizarre Sister Agnes words that they loved mocking. Agnes, the elegant nun.

"How *is* Timmy?"

"Timmy's—" Peg laughs. "Well, you know how *he* is. Always writing letters to invisible Dad and making paper airplanes out of them. Lately, though, it's this bee thing. He's really into bees. See, the toughest bee, he goes and gets this woman to screw—"

"Is this a joke?"

"No, this is how it happens, in *midair* too. So when he pulls out, he automatically just splits in half and dies. Isn't it gross?"

"It's sad."

"Anyway, the thing is, Timmy wants to check out these bees but they keep stinging him. He's been stung like fifteen times."

"Is he all right?"

"Timmy's fine. *I'd* have never broken up with him, Timmy's funny as hell."

The story makes Alex realize how things go on just the same without her. They must all be surfing by now. She notices that one of Peg's ankles is swollen, blue turning yellowish. But she doesn't want to make her have to explain how it happened, and she isn't all that curious anyhow.

"Hear that?" she asks, looking toward Roommate. "She's grinding her teeth all the time, drives me nuts."

"Maybe she's dreamin she's eatin."

"She's dreaming she's grinding her teeth."

Peg picks up the bag of chips, then changes her mind and puts them down again.

"Who's the guy with the crotch of his pants duck-taped?" she asks.

"Ya mean Alfred?"

"I dunno. He told me how to get to your room. He said you were the most normal person at Camden."

"Alfred?" Alex says. "That's funny."

"*He*'s funny, he was chewin a wad of paper. First I thought it was gum, but it was yellow. He was chewin a legal pad." Peg looks up at Alex and smiles big. "He's kinda cute."

"Alfred's gay," Roommate says, awake, stepping over Lars. "Who are you? Do you guys haveta be so noisy? What time is it? Janet's s'posed to buy me Chinese."

"Hi," Peg says. "I'm Peg."

Roommate starts brushing her hair, hard, then bends over and picks the nail scissors off the floor.

"How'd these get here?" She abandons the brush to cut her toenails. "I been looking for these."

"Why's Janet buying you Chinese?"

"A bet. I bet her she couldn't steal an entire place setting from food service—ya know, soup bowl, glass, the works."

"Why?"

"I was bored . . . she's always stealin shit anyhow."

"Great. Encourage her."

"Oh, lighten up, Alex, tell me you care."

Alex gives Peg a what-I-have-to-deal-with look and Peg makes a noise in her throat.

She looks nervous, something Alex has never seen. Peg afraid of Roommate? Peg, the one who walked into a liquor store at thirteen and came out with three free bottles of gin? Peg, who took fifty smacks with a ruler across her knuckles for writing obscene graffiti in the confessional and never flinched, not once? Peg, who instigated a riot in Girl Scouts, Ring Dings smushed in the heads of more than half a troop? She must just be tense, Alex thinks, from the drive.

"This is my old friend Peg," she tells Roommate.

"I see. Hi." Not very enthusiastic. "Just in time." Taking her shirt off, she stands in front of the open port-o-closet and stares in.

"In time for what?" Peg asks before Alex gets a chance.

"Dressed to Get Laid party . . . isn't that why you're here?" She gives her leg a self-congratulatory slap, then apologizes, still gazing into the closet, obviously still quite pleased with herself.

"Oh," Alex says, "I forgot."

Somehow, the conversation puts Peg in mind of Joe, though she doesn't remember his name. When she starts asking questions, Roommate gets all fake excited, pleading with Alex to let her answer.

"Go ahead," Alex says. "I don't give a shit."

"Alex found out he was wearing glasses only 'cause he thought he looked good in 'em, the guy's got perfect vision. Can you believe that?"

Roommate yelps and punches the port-o-closet door and skips around singing, "Joe the dud stud, Joe the dud stud," like a five-year-old.

Alex secretly thinks the name is clever but would never give her the satisfaction of looking amused.

"When I first heard that, I peed in my pants. Seriously."

Peg, with the sense to move on to another topic, says, "Got a bottle opener? Beer's gettin warm."

In the hall, Alex sees Ponzio leaning against his door. His hair looks unusually clean but he's stoned, sad.

"If I don't get an aspirin soon," he says, "I'll break the door down."

"Whatsamatter?"

"Oh, I don't know, I'm locked out. My mother just called. She wanted to know if I came by Philly today because when she got home the toilet seat was up. Came by Philly? Is she fucking out of it or what?"

"That's OK," Alex says. "My mother calls and asks where I am."

Ponzio brightens a little. Does an imitation of his mother that consists of somehow making a cigarette stick to his lip so that it bobs when he screeches, "Maybe it was the super! Darling, I simply hate the idea of the super using the toilet!" into a invisible phone.

"Shh," Alex says, "Lars is sleeping."

"Fuck him!" Ponzio yells, then, lowering his voice, "I *know* he's been using my toothpaste."

"Didya try gettin in the window?"

"Bolted."

"Call Security," Alex says. "I gotta pee."

In the stall she reads the ongoing graffiti. Every sentence is in a different handwriting.

"Read a poem and maybe cry awhile." Blue script.

"Don't write a page around it / Don't write a cage around it." Thick marker.

"Aren't you a freshman?" Scrawled pencil.

Then the latest, "Aren't you?" in what looks like eyeliner or chocolate. All the rest of the graffiti is old, except "I hate everything and want to love you with a knife," which has been updated: "fe" crossed out and changed to "sh." I want to love you with a knish.

No toilet paper and it's too late to get up and look for some. "Drip dry," Peg would say. Roommate'd be screaming her head off. She'd be sure to bring up "lack of consideration" at the next house meeting. Pulling up her pants, Alex is impatient to get back to Peg. With Peg, she's peed side by side on the beach. Backyards, if necessary. One time a guy drove up and caught them in his driveway. Chased them all around town, then couldn't think of anything to do with them once he caught up. Sometimes, she could really miss all that. Times like this, when her roommate has just woken up, Alex is reminded that Rockaway girls don't need toilet paper.

Back in the hall, Alex remembers about the bottle opener. Ponzio's still in the same spot, holding the dead ends of his long blond hair, a lot like Peg's hair, up close to his face.

"Didya call?"

"Yeah, they're coming. Got any aspirins?"

"Oh . . . yeah, I also haveta find a bottle opener."

"You *have* one," Ponzio says, following her to her room.

"I do?"

"Yeah, I saw one the other day, behind the dresser."

Alex doesn't bother asking what he was doing behind the dresser or why he left it there. Ponzio is probably her best friend, so these things slide.

"Dontcha knock?" Roommate says as they come through the door. "I could be naked."

"So could I," Ponzio says.

Not only is Roommate dressed but she's wearing Alex's

shirt. Ridiculously low neckline since she's a lot shorter, what some people might call "dainty."

Peg's a "big girl," but lean, muscular. She's of course wearing OP corduroy shorts and a Rockaway Beach Surf Shop T-shirt.

"Hello, hello," Ponzio says when Alex introduces him. "I saw you comin up the stairs, you looked kinda lost—surfer girl in the woods."

"Yeah, yeah," Peg says, "Miss Hawaiian." Alex appreciates that.

"Well, any friend of Alex's must be a lunatic." He sits next to her and lifts her hand. "It's in your palm."

"Sorry," Alex says, "but Alfred insists I'm the most normal person here."

"Where's she gonna sleep?" Roommate wants to know.

"If you were nice you'd sleep at Lars's."

"Larry's," corrects Roommate.

"Floor's fine," says Peg, no doubt uncomfortable, being spoken of as if she weren't there.

"Alfred owes me ten dollars," Ponzio says, then gets up and stands over Lars.

"Is he dead?"

"Fuck off," Roommate says.

Alex opens the beers and hands them out. Ponzio rolls a joint on top of *Coming of Age in Samoa* and hands it to Peg. She says she caught her brothers, ten and twelve, getting high in their boiler room.

"Guest of honor!" Ponzio exclaims, holding up a lit match. "You can sleep in my bed."

A small groan from Lars rolling over, probably hearing pot mentioned somewhere in the back of his brain.

Alex brings up the time the guy caught them peeing because she can't think of anything else to say. Peg remembers "only vaguely," but tells Alex about the electrocution on the wave machine at Action Park's grand opening, how they're planning to ban radios on some beaches, that huge barges are sucking sand from the ocean bottom to spit back on the shore, and, oh yeah, Bean bit off some guy's nose in a fight.

"How can you bite off someone's nose?" Roommate says. "It's impossible."

"I think it was just a big piece."

"Disgusting," Ponzio says, then, "Look, here's Janet."

"Bingo!" yelps Janet, pouncing on the joint. "Sorry I'm late." She takes a deep drag, tries to talk and hold in smoke at the same time. She's got on an orange vinyl dress. "I've been up for like three days, it's gettin seriously weird . . . Don't I look terrible? Who told Lars he could sleep? Who are you?"

"Peg," Peg says.

"You're the girl who Ponzio's always yakkin about, from—wait, lemme guess—Cleveland, no, Denver? I'm Janet. Which Chinese place should we go to? Would someone else drive? I think I'm beginning to hallucinate."

"How can you *think* you're hallucinating?" Roommate says. "Either you are or you aren't."

"Oh . . . Ponzio," Janet says, "I didn't tell you, Security's out there lookin for you. You get caught stealin from the bookstore or somethin?"

"Holy shit." Ponzio's running out the door. "I forgot."

"He forgot he stole something?"

"You're the klepto," Roommate says. "*He's* student council president."

"What's that got to do with anything?"

"*He's* student council president," Peg asks, "with spikes?"

"A respectable klepto would be able to steal a measly coupla dishes," says Janet.

"Yeah, time to collect. Eat, eat, eat—you guys wanna come?"

"No thanks," Alex says, grateful for Peg. Otherwise she might actually be spending the evening with these two.

"Well, see ya at the party then." Roommate kneels by Peg, whispering, "Go after Alfred, it's the only challenge left around here." Then to Alex, "Tell Larry where I went, maybe I'll bring him an egg roll."

Janet finds this hilarious and the two squeal out the door.

"Did she mean gay guys were the only challenge left?" Peg asks. "God, I'd rather be a nun."

The thought enters Alex's mind that maybe Joe is gay. Maybe Joe wouldn't sleep with her because he's gay. But that seems too good to be true and anyway she's stopped caring. The glasses only topped it all off. "Did you notice Janet's eyebrow?" she asks Peg.

"Why would I?"

"It's almost gone, that's why. The girl gets so fucking neurotic doing her thesis that she rubs and rubs at her eyebrow. I'm tellin you, she's rubbin her eyebrow completely off."

"Bullshit."

"I swear it." Alex gives the old Girl Scout's honor sign, something they've done since the Ring Ding incident, when they both got thrown out. "She's writing her thesis on the religious movement of Jerry Garcia."

"Cool."

"Man, Peg, you been in Rockaway *too* long."

Peg just stares at her, then down at the floor, makes a circle with a sneaker in a pile of dust. Alex feels mean—how could she say that? Confused—having the upper hand for the first time. Embarrassed—how could anyone think a thesis on the Grateful Dead was cool?

Luckily, Ponzio returns. "He was here and left and I hadda call again. Janet's out to lunch." He lights the half-smoked joint lying on the floor.

"No, she's out to dinner," Peg says, but the joke doesn't go over too well.

"Yum," Ponzio says. "Now we have Lars baby all to ourselves."

They stand over the bed and pass the joint around. Lars has got one knee up to his chest, the other leg straight out, and his arms in a similar pattern. The outstretched hand, flopping over the side, looks as if it's pointing at the pile of stuff on the floor near Alex's bed. His mouth is open.

"How can he be comfortable like that?"

"He doesn't know he's not comfortable because he's asleep."

"He must be exhausted."

"He's twitching."

"Maybe he stayed up all night with Janet."

"What a scandal."

"Maybe he's only pretending he's asleep so that he doesn't have to go eat Chinese."

"Maybe he wants to hear what we've got to say about him."

Knock at the door. "Come in!" in unison—Alex, Ponzio, and, oddly enough, Lars, stirring.

The Security man sticks his head in.

"Someone need their door opened?"

"Yeah," Ponzio says. "God bless you."

"Smells good in here." The Security man sniffs dramatically and closes the door behind Ponzio.

Lars's eyes are open, but it doesn't seem as if he's seeing anything. Still, they move over to Alex's side of the room. Peg's eyes haven't left the door and Alex knows she's wondering about the pot.

"Don't worry," she tells her. "They got people slittin their wrists up, breakin windows, ya know, settin off *fire extinguishers*? They like potheads, we're sedate. . . . Mornin, Lars, everyone's graduated, you missed it."

Lars says, "I feel like shit. Both my hands are asleep."
Then he jumps up, blinking. Four jumping jacks, a deep knee
bend, and a couple of jogs in place on the bed. Alex notices
he has an erection. Peg tells a story about her father, who
wakes the whole house at six doing exercises to Herb Alpert
and the Tijuana Brass. Lars collapses back on the bed and
shuts his eyes.

"Feel better?" Ponzio asks from the doorway.

"Oh," Alex says. "Your aspirins, I forgot."

"You read my mind," says Lars.

"Not you."

"That's OK," Ponzio says, "headache's gone."

"Me, me," says Lars. "Please? . . . And a beer?"

"Me too," says Peg, and Alex starts searching through her
underwear drawer for the bottle, thinks maybe she'll take
some herself.

Dinner's skipped, beer and chips replenished, then the
shower lineup—Peg, Ponzio, Alex, Lars. Ponzio, annoyed that
Lars has to come to *their* dorm to shower, suggests cutting
out while he's in there. OK, says Alex, as long as they leave
a note. The note's not out of any sort of allegiance but because she's thinking ahead. The wrath of Lars, not to mention Roommate.

After the shower, she puts on Roommate's favorite shirt
even though she doesn't particularly like it, even though it
doesn't fit all that great. It's Peg's idea. Then the three of
them walk outside, onto the lawn. Long dusk shadows and
lilac smell. A scene that'd sell the school.

"This is the only place I've ever been in my life where
the hippies can't play hacky sack," Ponzio says as they
approach the people, ball, Frisbee traffic. Elvis Costello
blares out some window, hard to tell which, with the sound

bouncing from one house to another. Two neat rows of white houses that could make Camden look, to a stranger, to Peg, like a Quaker settlement or a home for unwed mothers.

But her face has other thoughts on it—so open, like awe or envy. Alex, who's always aspired to be Peg (beautiful, aggressive, carefree), is caught completely off guard, assures herself she's imagining.

Ponzio imitates the Elvis Costello stance. Like a chicken. They all dance and sing along in funny voices. But since all anyone knows is the chorus, they lose interest. Ponzio and Alex start up some shoe golf.

It's a game they invented themselves. Who can kick his shoe off the farthest, then the highest. That's the warm-up. Then a course is set. Stumps, chairs, whatever, for targets. It's no problem, since most of the houses have moved the living-room furniture outside.

Peg is distracted from the game, keeps looking around. Still, she's winning by seven or eight points. The punk rockers, she says, look especially weird against the backdrop: mountains, farmland, miles of open, crooked fields. "Like someone shipped 'em all out here for a photo session. Mod vs. Wilderness, what a concept." Alex knows that from now on she won't be able to see them any other way.

"At Kingsborough," Peg goes on, "it could look like an ad for beer, but here, man, it's strictly perfume or sunglasses or hair gel."

In a way, Alex thinks, Alfred was right. Maybe in Rockaway they think she's strange, but here she's normal as hell. The only one here she knows of whose parents are still together, who even likes her parents. The only one without a single pair of black pants.

"I'll bet all these people have trust funds," says Peg.

· · ·

Three people at the Dressed to Get Laid party have already told Alex they like her shirt. The last was a six-foot girl in four-inch pumps, yanking a guy in a leather G-string around on a leash. She also informed Alex that the party was "technically" named Revenge of Dressed to Get Laid since "traditionally" it was annual and there'd already been one last semester.

Alex doesn't need to be reminded of last semester's party. Last semester she spent the whole night waiting for Joe to show and avoiding a visiting painting professor whom she'd made the mistake of sleeping with the night before.

James? John? Joseph? yes, Joseph made her sit for hours while he held slides of his work up to a bare lightbulb. He fucked like he was stabbing her.

Afterwards, she tried telling herself she'd learned something. Something about professors, strangers, maybe even a little something about painting. But the next night, at the party—where she sat on the stairs listening to Roommate develop tactics to make Lars jealous, and got hungry, fed up, stepped on—she realized what it really was she'd learned: Displaced longing is a bad thing. She cried some, sometime either before or after she and Roommate, huddled on the dorm kitchen floor, ate two frozen pizzas, only half cooked, because they were too impatient to wait.

Peg is talking to Joe. For a long time they've been talking—well, yelling, which you've got to do, to be heard. The music's noise—Sex Pistols, Dead Kennedys, Fleshtones. More exposed flesh than at a beach, she thinks, remembering how Joe recognized Peg from Rockaway right away, while Peg pretended to take a minute, place the face. Flirtatiousness? Loyalty? Alex couldn't tell, couldn't care less. Drinking since seven, dancing since they got here, laughing, laughing since Ponzio pointed out the Brazilian. How he's circling the room, looking left out.

She follows Ponzio off the dance floor, toward the bar. He's still dancing as he waits in line. When it's his turn to order, he swivels his body to ask what color condom she'd like. Free condoms if you buy two drinks at once.

It's got to be a joke. No one actually gets laid at Dressed to Get Laid, do they? It'd be embarrassing. How could you possibly face the person the next day? And more than that, how could you feel any less turned on, any more repulsed than after *this*?

"The purpose"—she's testing her new theory on Ponzio—"the purpose is to make fun of all the other parties. If you wanna dress up, you can make fun of yourself."

It sounds good, but neither of them is totally convinced. Still, it's not at all like last semester. She's happy. "What's the difference *why?*" she tells him. "I just am." And she notices how anxious the Brazilian seems about Joe, as though he's a bodyguard. His midriff T-shirt shows an outy belly button and says, "Good Under the Hood," an ad for Valvoline oil.

What if he's in love with Joe? Of course, of course he is, that's it. Ponzio pats her head, calls her a dumb freshman for ever believing otherwise. "You'd think Rockaway was devoid of gays."

"It is. Some come from outside, but they mostly go to the beach and go home."

"Mostly?"

"Well, there's shitheads who get restless. Guys go down with baseball bats, ya know, fag bashing, smear the queer, dead meat." All words that belong in someone else's mouth—Sloane's, Bean's, Lefty's. "Is Joe gay then? I'm just a dumb freshman, I don't know."

"No," Ponzio says, "I doubt it. Virgin maybe, but not gay." He stops a guy walking past and asks for a cigarette. The guy's got a flashlight around his neck, the significance of which Alex would rather not think about. A virgin? She really doesn't want to think about that either. Decides to go back and dance. Ponzio calls after her, "You're not dumb, ya know. Just a little green."

In the red light, everyone looks seedy. There's a porno movie flickering on the ceiling above the dance floor. Woman with enormous tits doing all kinds of things to a man—hairy, faceless—which someone has interspersed with footage of Camden students standing on a lawn and pointing.

Alex has to dance vertically since the room is so full. Fishnets, garters, transparent lingerie. Where do these girls get the stuff? The boys, they're a lot more practical. Bathrobes, or towels, loincloths, underwear, or nothing at all.

But all of it's funny now. Bodies falling from the sky, from this guy with a mattress strapped to his back, giving rides. After a while, nothing matters. Not the video camera in the corner, not the smell—beer, sweat, cigarettes—not the stain on Roommate's shirt—colliding, slipping, twirling some nerd from her International Relations class, around, around, around, till he looks sick. Nothing can possibly matter except moving. Moving matters.

Janet is pulling her by the wrist, off the dance floor. "You're a fucking robot, aren't you tired yet?" Not answering, Alex slumps against the wall, feels *heat*. Like it's coming from the inside out.

"Get up!" Janet says. "Where's Ponzio? His girlfriend's in a fight."

"What?"

"That girl from your room."

Alex pushes through the crowd.

"Wait for me!" yells Janet. "I think she's winning, though."

Alex has to giggle. Peg is being held back by Joe, the Brazilian, *and* Ponzio. Three men to hold her back, it's classic. A girl wearing a leopard skin screams "Dyke!" and paces a small cleared area. Her nose is streaming blood and her hair sticks straight up. Janet finds it necessary to let Alex know that the girl's hair was like that before the fight.

"Let's go." Alex holds Peg's arm, still giggling. It's hard not to. The boys move away, except Ponzio, who guides Peg toward the door. She's sort of limping. When she passes the girl she looks as if she wants to spit but her mouth's too dry or she hasn't the energy, mumbles "Witch" instead.

"Hi, Alex," Joe says as they walk out. Everyone's watching them. "Bye, Alex."

They sit on the lawn and smoke pot. Some difficulty getting the story out of Peg, who's lying on the grass, perfectly still except for her forearm, which periodically lifts to pass the joint.

"From what I saw," Ponzio says, "it was something about her boyfriend. You know that guy, shaved eyebrows and 'Understand the Soviets' written across his chest? Well, I guess he took a piss from the top of the stairs, over the railing, and got Peg by accident. I don't know what the girl has to do with it."

"I called him disgusting," Peg finally offers. "I called him a creep, reject, retard—I mean it *was* disgusting."

"And?"

"And I don't wag my tail for no one. No one calls *me* a dyke. She calls me a dyke, I'm not gonna sit around thinkin up more names."

"That's it?" Alex is laughing, almost proud. "That's all? *Bor-ing.* Ya sure that's it?"

But Peg is snoring, and the joint in her hand, stretched toward Alex, has gone out.

In the morning, Ponzio's gone and Peg's up before Alex, shaking her awake with one foot. Her hands rotate over each

other in circles, a lifeguard signal meaning "We need a reel
out here."

"Ya know," she says, smiling, "I thoughta somethin. Up
close, spring's not all *that* great ... up close it's kinda
crawly, kinda sticky. Let's eat. I'm itchin to get back and
check the waves."

11 | CRUISE TO NOWHERE

Besides Alicia McHenry, brownnose cashier, and that chick from the A train, Timmy has not been with a girl in close to six months. It's too much hassle, at first, having to tell about yourself, where you work, where you hang out, what sign, like a test. Meanwhile, keeping up the flirt. It's too much hassle sneaking them in his house, where half the time a nun is sleeping.

So he's just taking a break for a while. That's what he's telling Chowderhead anyway. "I'm just taking a break."

They are unloading cases of Schlitz in the back of Mickey's Deli, trying to figure out what to do with Timmy's extra ticket for Cruise to Nowhere. He invited Alex but she said no.

"Ya don't take breaks from sex," insists Chowderhead, grunting. He grunts every time he puts down a case, as a joke.

"I've decided to be a priest," Timmy says, and "Da ya think we could nab a case a this?"

Chowder says he hates Schlitz, then does his imitations of Father O'Leary. Cross-eyed, walking in circles, beating a ruler against his leg.

Sometimes Timmy can't tell if he remembers Father O'Leary himself or if it's just Chowder's imitation, alive since second grade, that stays. And watching it now he realizes that the mimicry really has nothing at all to do with Father O'Leary but instead has to do with Timmy and Chowder and all the other times the imitation's been done. This has never occurred to him before.

"Father Timmy Ray Maggot!" Chowder laughs.

Timmy crosses himself and lies down on the storeroom floor. Summer's here. It's their last day of storeroom slavery.

"See," Chowder says. "Without sex, you've lost your ability to unload."

"What!?" Timmy jumps up.

They race to see who can unload more cases in a minute. Timmy. Then who can spit the farthest. Chowder. Then it's lunchtime. Long break, since the boss is on jury duty.

They go around the corner to Ciro's Pizza, even though they could also go to the The Original Ciro's across the street, and even though Chowder has a bologna sandwich from home.

Alicia McHenry joins them, without asking if she can come along, then bitches for a half-hour about getting sauce on her shirt. Shiny, low-cut, white with an orange grease stain above the nipple.

She wants Timmy to ask her to Cruise to Nowhere, that's obvious. So they try not to mention it, talk about who's the best pitcher, Gooden or Valenzuela, and Famous Bartenders School, where Timmy and Chowder now go, taking the A train to Manhattan two nights a week.

Timmy and Chowder wolf three slices each and Alicia eats part of one, pulling the cheese off first with long fingernails painted sauce color. Too much. She says they'll have to give her special treatment when they get to be bartenders, "Raffle tickets and buy-backs." She offers to pay for the Cokes.

Then work again. The afternoon is cool, gray, perfect for sleeping. They hang around the empty store listening to the radio. Occasionally, Chowderhead scratches at an instant lottery ticket with his teeth. Alicia sings the choruses to songs she likes, "Glamorous Life" and "Cruel Summer," and dances a little over by the produce. Her dancing used to kind of turn Timmy on, before he slept with her, but now he's glad she's way the hell on the other side of the store. Tonight, he'll go down to Sheepshead Bay, early, and scalp the extra ticket.

First customer of the afternoon is a woman, leather coat and what Chowder calls "the divorced look." She buys tampons and dog food and smiles at Timmy even though Chowder is working the register. Timmy ignores her, goes on reading an engrossing article. Seems these molested children were overheard singing, "I can see who you are / You're a naked movie star."

When the woman is gone, Chowder has this very serious expression on his face, he's telling Timmy, "This is no joke, she was very hot. Definite storeroom action. Whatsamatter, man?"

"Timmy's just takin a break, remember?" calls Alicia McHenry from produce.

"It's not still Alex," Chowder says. "You're whipped."

"Alex who?" asks Alicia, all innocence.

"Mind ya business," says Chowder.

Timmy cannot stand the name Alex in Alicia's heavy Brooklyn accent. Neither could Alex, if she heard, he just knows it.

"Ask someone to go on the cruise," Chowder says. "You're almost a bartender. I'd even let ya take my sister."

"No thanks," Timmy says. "Cruise to Nowhere with no one."

But they've gotten him thinking about Alex again. Alex with him on the Cruise to Nowhere. Alex sitting at a bar that he's tending, and bending her long neck forward slightly so he can see that mystery place where the breasts begin. Tonight was the night to start off the summer right. Lifeguarding season, goodbye to Mickey's. But Alex said, "No. I don't think so."

"Peg likes you," Chowder says. "Call up Peg."

"What for?"

"It'll make me happy."

Timmy picks up the phone.

"474-9323. While I was seein her, she was always yakkin about you." Timmy knows this isn't true but he's curious how Peg's doing. They should have told her when they went to buy the tickets. While the phone rings, he's thinking what a schemer Chowder is. Motives or no motives. And he hopes they'll be friends for a long time. When they're as old as all the men in Duffy's, when—

"Hello."

"Oh hi, is Chow—Peg there."

"I'm Peg."

"Hi, it's Timmy."

"Timmy! What's up!"

"Nothing much . . . I was like wondering what you're doing tonight. . . ."

"Goin out with Timmy."

"Timmy who?"

"You, stupid." She giggles this very sexy giggle, then stops it short. Timmy can hear some sort of gurgling in the background.

"Um, I got this extra ticket to Cruise to Nowhere, ya know, gambling boat thing."

"Wow, when, what time?"

"Six-thirty?"

"Great. I'll pick you up. I just got a car."

"Really? OK. And Chowder too?"

"Sure."

"Great, bye."

"Wait, dontcha wanna know what kind?"

"What kind?"

"Car, stupid."

"Sure."

"Subaru," Peg says. "Blue."

"Cool. See ya."

"Bye."

He hangs up, announces it was a breeze.

"Now!" Chowder claps his hands together. "I'll follow you around all night incognito and make sure things don't get too innocent."

In the next two hours, Timmy, feeling very energetic, does a crossword and a half, mops the floor, collects the stale Entenmann's boxes to return, and even tells Alicia McHenry that she has a good voice. It's funny how effortless things seem when you make the effort. Really something.

. . .

He's a real nowhere man
Sitting in his nowhere land
Making all his nowhere plans for nobody. . . .

Between the boat noise, wind, and shouting, they can sing as loud as they want and the sound will stay tiny, floating away. And no one sings louder or softer than anyone else, not even Alicia McHenry, who Chowder invited at the last minute when his date canceled. It's Peg who started them. Peg, already a little stoned when she picked them up but still in top form, is now swearing she'll jump overboard at the slightest decline in fun.

Doesn't have a point of view
Knows not where he's going to
Isn't he a bit like you and me-e-e. . . .

She hangs on Timmy's waist and throws potato chips overboard, specks in the black, then whispers to Alicia McHenry, some girl stuff probably. About him? Chowderhead? About when they're going to make a run to the john together?

He's waiting for the boat to reach the twenty-mile mark, or wherever it is they can begin gambling. He has fifty-six dollars, mostly in ones, in a ball at the bottom of his pocket.

Alicia tries to get them to sing "Nowhere Over the Rainbow" but no one is into it.

Timmy wins big. Five hundred bucks. The roulette wheel. The numbers from Alex's dog's registration tag. She had given them to him. When she turned down the ticket, he asked for some numbers and that's what she'd given him.

So beers are on him, singing old Scrapy's lucky. He gets to tell Alex that old Scrapy's lucky and take her to . . . dinner. Hee hee, Alicia stood the whole night in front of *one* slot machine. Chain-smoking. Her hair looks like a plastic helmet, exactly, and Peg swears that Alicia said herself that she zippers her pants with a wrench.

Chowder has broken even. So he'll stop now. Time to get drunk on Timmy's money. The summer is coming, is here! He's so psyched, he says, he can't sit still. And "There'll be waves tomorrow. I just know it."

Peg says there are never any waves, ever, and pulls Timmy away, out onto the deck.

"Let's chew the breeze."

"You mean shoot."

"That, too. Oh, I don't know what to do about him."

"Who? Chowder?" But Timmy knows.

"We just can't seem to hang out efficiently." She squints and begins counting her money. "And we're s'posed to be partners again." She's down forty dollars. "Remember last summer that horn, Patrick something? The short guy who always smelled like Ben-Gay?"

"O'Neill."

"Maybe O'Ryan—anyway, one day I was sittin in the shack and he comes runnin up asking for a *jetty wrench. A jetty wrench!* Chowder sent him to ask me for a *jetty wrench.*"

Her face flushes, seems to open up.

"I mean, he did that just for me, to make *me* laugh, ya know?"

Timmy nods and doesn't tell her he's heard the story before. It's such a nice night. Money. Stars. A good buzz on. He wants to laugh when Peg asks, "How come Chowder doesn't call me up no more? Alicia?" Instead he kisses her.

She doesn't object. It's easy. He thinks of all the old times (real old, pre-Alex), back in his showerhouse, where they hid *The Happy Hooker* and read aloud in between bouts of mad sex with their clothes on.

Remembering this, he thinks how Peg seems more like a relative than someone he just wants to sleep with. He once put jellyfish down her bathing suit when she was like nine years old. She's someone like Chowderhead, even knows Father O'Leary. How could he forget?

He considers asking about Alex and that Joe guy, but he's too happy. All he can do is kiss her, keep kissing her, kissing her.

LIMBO | 12

Close to thirty people were standing on the sandbar when it busted. Thirty heads and arms sucked up, out with the riptide. That was a thing to see. Something for the eyes, all that orange at once, so many guards, still not enough. And everyone down to look, as if it had been announced on a PA beforehand.

The crowd was quiet for a crowd. No one knew what to say. It got so bad, seven or eight swimmers would be trying to hang on each guard at once. It got so you couldn't tell who was calling for help anymore: lifeguard, swimmer, or some poor relative on the shore. All this Alex has missed, overhears and pumps out of strangers. It is too much to believe.

She stands on the wall, vending apron still on and holding a can of Diet Pepsi. She'll hear it back at work, taking an hour for lunch when everyone's just itching to get down there, take a look.

She's looking at a human chain. Bodies linking up to search—for who? The leader (looks like Artie or his brother, Mac) shouts "Dive!"

Dive. Three strokes ahead. Surface. Back one stroke

length. Dive. Three strokes. Surface. Back one. Dive, again and again. The simplest, most elegant of water ballets seems to go on for hours. In reality, maybe five, ten minutes at the most.

And then it's Peg, God, Peg who finds the body. Alex can hear her wail all the way from the wall, and she thinks how hard it must be, keeping the girlness in. To dive down and feel, actually feel a tiny arm or heel like just another piece of trash and not scream, faint, puke. To drag it out, blow in it, pound, plead, pound. All the while knowing. In front of everyone, knowing.

Now the crowd circles the little blue body and Alex can't see anything anymore except right in front of her, where a pigeon limps and pokes holes in a slice of ham. She realizes she has been holding her breath, the Diet Pepsi dropped, foaming on the sand.

To the left, down a few yards, she spots Timmy's tiny mom and Agnes, crossing themselves vigorously, a violent sign language. Red in the face. The nun no doubt extremely uncomfortable in those thick robes.

Sirens. Sounding too high, something screwy, the mechanism or her ears. And it must be one hundred degrees out here. Helicopters and the Coast Guard and, shit, Peg. Is it Peg who lost the kid? Lost and found? Poor thing, dying like that before the fireworks even started.

Why? Does Sister Agnes even *wonder* why? Alex, trying to follow the nun's gaze, sees a wavy horizon line and the one visible landmass, which she'd grown up believing was Europe but is really New Jersey. What does Agnes see out there? Babies go directly to limbo, but what about children? What is there for children?

Bells from the Good Humor truck are weirdly amplified. Dry throat, and a feeling like being too high, useless.

She knows she should be back at work. Scooping hot dogs from the brown puddle in the metal compartment. A lot sold on the Fourth of July, especially a hot one like this. On a hot one like this, there isn't a soul who doesn't want Italian ice, knish, relish. Everyone using the money they never have time to spend so that Mr. Zuckoff, her boss, can get rich.

In Rockaway, there are lots like Zuckoff who gamble on the weather. And it's true, the sky can make or break them, at the very least keep them drunk, warm, full. Today is a miracle draw, they're all pleased to death. Today is a perfect July Fourth.

Maybe he'll let her off easy, raking in as he is, but Big Tom, minding the stand till she relieves him, Big Tom, he'll have something to say. Still, being gone so long, she can't go back without details. The complete story, names and everything.

People are saying it's the barge's fault. The barge working on the beach-replacement project pulled out too quick, caused the riptide, which broke the jetty. The jetty swarming with swimmers. But no one is really sure. The barge pulls in and out every day. It's mainly a place for the blame. Can't very well take nature to court.

Sister Agnes looks pained, something in her foot. Without removing her shoe, she cradles it, rocks her foot in her hand. The robes, black against the sand, black against the striped umbrellas, white towels, white of her face—it's like a movie Alex once saw or something from a dream. But there should be a breeze for her robes to flutter in. There should be a soundtrack.

Alex jumps off the wall to move closer. A circle of age spots on the old nun's wrist seems to twist, spin, in the horrible glare. And what at first Alex hears as a wheeze she realizes is a prayer. Grainylike, and soft, aimed straight up, high up in the air. I ought to help her with the piece of glass or wood, whatever it is, in her foot, Alex thinks, but she is too scared, can't interrupt.

Timmy's mother mutters along. There are big stains of sweat on the flowered dress and she's punching her own legs. Are they praying in words even? There must be some appropriate saint that the sister knows to call on. There must be some jerk who drowned himself for Jesus and got his portrait painted, got written up and prayed to. Nuns *could* do something useful. If only they swam, knew first aid, if only they'd quit hiding a body that works, they might help, they might—

"Hey, Alex. Heavy shit, huh?"

It's Sloane, dripping wet, a link from the chain. He's hopping, knocking at the side of his head to get the water out of his ear.

"Sloane! Tell me what's going on."

Sister Agnes, turning, says nothing.

"Nothing now. It's over now."

"What's over—what happened?"

"You mean you don't know?"

"Not the whole thing."

"God."

"Tell me."

"You really don't know?"

"Oh, shit."

"What?"

"Well, it's Timmy."

Agnes is chanting louder.

"What? . . . Sloane, what?"

"He lost the kid."

"What?"

"He was the only one to lose one."

"What?"

"Six-year-old spic, a girl."

"Timmy?"

"Listen, I gotta go to sleep. I'm gonna pass out."

"No. You're gonna tell me first." She clutches at his arm. Maybe the first time she's ever willingly touched Sloane.

"He was haulin two kids in and some panicky old guy starts pullin his hair underwater, then just pulled one of the kids right off his shoulder. Grabbed on to Timmy and wouldn't let go." Sloane either laughs or coughs. "Can't blame the guy really."

"But what else? What happened?"

"Well, *I* dragged ten of 'em back."

"To Timmy. What happened to him?"

"He swam in." Sloane will not look at her. "He left the kid and swam in."

And then, before Alex can ask any more—the Media People, vans of them, pouring out onto the beach. Panting, babbling, cursing the heat, pointing fingers, pointing cameras, banging into each other, and closing in on Alex and Sloane. She's trapped. Questions. Metal. She's stuck. Something's beeping. She's got to get out. She's got to squeeze through. Oh, Timmy, where are you? Behind Alex, Sloane seems happy to be swallowed up by the mob.

Mrs. Ray looks up. A small angry face but eyes turning velvety like Timmy's as Alex drops down next to her on the sand, as her hand reaches out and strokes Alex's hair. It's a chewed-up looking hand but feels cool and bony. Nice. Only Alex can't say so. Her nose runs. Her tongue is a big, dry rock.

Agnes is trembling. Agnes is finally removing her shoe. Dark splotches seep through the stocking. And Mrs. Ray is whispering that old story again. Is it true? Alex never really knew. When Timmy was a baby his ears bled.

13 | THE MURDERERS' CLUB

There's no way out of the Murderers' Club. Mouth-to-mouth, CPR, prayer—give it up. Once the ticket's bought, party's for you. Nicknames like "Butterfingers" stick.

For a while there, Chowderhead actually considered hiding Timmy in his attic. He'd just go back to the others and say that Timmy had split. No finding him anywhere.

But who'd believe that? No one. And besides, the attic is only dust, squirrels, insulation. Nothing to cheer a guy up. Nothing to prepare a guy to appear in front of the Parks Department for a mandatory judicial hearing.

Chowder sits on the Rays' old bashed-in milk box and tries to come up with something to say. "It'll blow over." "Cheer up." "Could happen to anyone." He knows he's supposed to say "I'm sorry," and that'd be OK if he just knew what it meant. Apologizing for someone else's fuck-up. There's enough to feel guilty about already. No need to drag other people in. No doubt Timmy is right now saying he's sorry to the dead kid, apologizing for being alive.

What did Chowder do? Nothing. Wasn't even there, with the day off to buy fireworks down in Chinatown and slide around Washington Square, try to find some decent smoke.

It isn't his fault that he came home like normal. It isn't his fault that nothing was left but the story, a serious-looking riptide, and an order: Make sure Timmy shows up at his Death Keg.

There'll be no questions asked. A frown at the most. Tradition says what to do; you aren't supposed to think about it. Tradition is people doing things over and over till they don't have to think about it. A sort of elaborate habit. Naturally Timmy should be treated like all those before him. Like a murderer.

So what's the problem? Why can't he get himself to move from the milk box? Watching a slug move toward his sneaker, Chowder considers how last year, maybe last week even, missing an event as big as this (thirty people almost drowning at once) would've completely pissed him off. Thirty chances for commendations, pictures in the paper, and those things girls automatically give to heroes.

But suddenly, everything's upside down. He's seeing himself like one of those people who wish for dysentery so they'll lose weight. Missing the point when it's everywhere. Is it luck? fate? that kept him out of it? How long can he just sit here? And why not quit lifeguarding altogether? Quit killing fly nests in the dilapidated trailer shack, eating polluted clams, sleazing around downtown, quit shit beer and jumping off bridges?

He'd almost forgotten. Independence Day is the annual jump of the Brass Balls Bridge Jumpers Association. Those same assholes forcing him to get Timmy to the Death Keg will be jumping off a sixty-foot bridge at two a.m., himself included.

Several times he stands and approaches the door. Several times sits down again. An ice cream truck bends around the corner. Screaking brakes drown out the lonely bell song. Kids are hanging on with their whole bodies, shrieking, pumped up for the Fourth of July. The holiday of no church, no required kissing, no shoes. Sugar instead. Frozen sugar and exploding color and free run of the world, your entire block.

The truck stops in front of Timmy's house and all the kids jump off and fight to be first in line. In the chaos, someone's quarter gets knocked away and it comes rolling toward Chowder's feet, just missing the slug, who still has a good eight inches to go. It seems to be getting dark incredibly slowly.

"Didya see my quarter?" says this shiny-skinned girl, hopping from one foot to the other. Chowder covers the quarter with his Pro-Ked.

"No, I didn't see any quarter."

"Well, ya got one then, please, mister?" She leans into him, smelling of barbecue, mosquito repellent.

"Whataya gonna buy with it?"

"Chocolate-chip fudge crunch," she says, sucking on her lip, twisting around to look back at the truck between each word.

"Why not ices? Don't ya like ices? It's so hot."

"Not allowed. Please, mister, he's gonna go away. *Please?*" Still hopping.

"You gotta pee?"

She stops bouncing, now ready to cry. Chowder moves his foot and points at the coin.

"Hey, look here, look at that, a quarter?" But the kid bursts anyhow. Picks up the quarter, yeah, but bawls all the way back to the truck.

He feels shitty. Like one of those horrible old men who take candy out of kids' ears, assuming it makes them happy. He wants to smush the slug, slide the smushed slug along the flagstone till it's unrecognizable. Instead he gets up and rings the bell. Usually he just walks right in, but the occasion seems formal.

"Oh, you," Mrs. Ray says and steps back to let him pass. Then, "Isn't it terrible?"

"Yes, yes, it is. I'm so sorry."

Jesus, hardly through the door and he's already said it. Realizing at once that it's something for other people, not a phrase you're supposed to mean. That's cool. He even says it again, sort of testing it out.

"I'm really sorry."

"Well." Mrs. Ray sighs. "What's done's done," and, "You can go on up, but I'll warn you, his room looks like it's been stirred up with a stick."

Chowder is relieved to be excused and takes the stairs two at a time, but at the top he gauges wrong. Lifts his leg too high for a stair that doesn't exist. Embarrassing, though no one sees.

The hallway is dark but Chowder knows the layout. Light comes from under Timmy's door, stretching itself out on the carpet. He knocks. Nothing. Then again. Nothing. So he goes in, not about to wait out there forever.

Mrs. Ray was not kidding. Furniture all rearranged, a bowl of soup obviously flung across the room with noodles still stuck to the wallpaper. That kiddie wallpaper Timmy's always had. Red, white, and blue ball players, frozen in various action poses. But besides that, it looks as if every piece of clothing Timmy owns is heaped in one place. Like Chowder's sister's room used to look before she went out on a date, from that endless trying on and taking off. Only the ant farm on the windowsill is where it's supposed to be. Tedious little ant world.

But no Timmy. Chowder wishes he had asked the little girl her name; reminded now of the nameless lost kid he hid out with for hours one night last summer. He still wonders why he did it and why the kid never once came to visit him.

Another Puerto Rican boy wandered up just yesterday, but weepy, fat Hector was not at all interesting. Also lost and waiting in the shack was this old lady Lefty found, and when Hector's huge family arrived, they decided to take her home with them—what's one more? They said they'd bring her by sometime next week.

Chowder walks to the window and looks out at the beach. Then straight down onto the balding lawn. Back to the beach, where the lighthouse is almost visible. Soon fireworks, soon the Death Keg.

So what the hell is he stalling for? Every new pause too purposeful because, secretly, Chowder hopes he'll never find him. Hopes Timmy has cut out hours ago and is on his way somewhere, anywhere far.

He kicks a pile of papers as he paces. They splatter across the floor. Postcards, all of 'em. All of 'em from Alex. Some are familiar because Timmy has read them aloud. But there's a lot more. Written in colored markers, sloppy script. He wonders what it'd be like to have a girlfriend for more than two weeks at a time or even someone who sent him regular mail, and he can't remember ever writing a letter in his life besides forged notes from his mother to some nun or other.

They're sure tempting, but it's wrong to read them. If Timmy should come in, then what? And it's crazy, but the ball players on the wallpaper are watching him. All the ants in the ant farm are watching him. This extremely average room is giving him the creeps.

So he leaves, goes to look in the bathroom. Finds Timmy naked, in an empty tub.

"Hi," Chowder says. "Are you all right?"

"Real gritty, real gritty."

Chowderhead sits on the edge.

"Why don't you get some water going, you'll feel better."

"The soap's fulla sand and it scratches." Timmy almost whines, almost laughs. He is making Chowder nervous.

"Get a holda yourself, man."

"Yeah," Timmy says, leaning to turn on the water. "It's OK." He puts the half-empty shampoo under the faucet. Then he throws it in Chowder's face, bottle and all.

"What the hell—"

"Where the fuck were you!? You're bullshit. What the hell do you know. You suck. Where the fuck were you!?"

This is something Chowder has not prepared himself for. His eyes sting, part shampoo, part tears, it's hard to tell.

"My day off." All he can get out.

"Well, fuck you."

"Well, fuck you."

Chowder moves, sits on the sink and rubs his eyes with his shirt. The water runs. Neither of them speaks until the bathtub's full and overfull, spilling on the floor.

"You better turn it off," Chowder says.

"Yeah, well, who asked you?"

"You're makin a mess, that's all."

The shock of finding Timmy in an empty tub has worn off, and Chowder is becoming kind of angry. Timmy is blaming the wrong person.

"A mess?" he's asking. "What do you mean?"

"A puddle, a flood if you let it go."

"Oh. Think it could get that bad?" Timmy laughs for an unnaturally long time, then turns dead serious.

"I hate water," he says. "Fuck."

Something's up downstairs. Chowder turns off the faucet to hear better. No protests. Timmy's shivering. It only takes a second to place the voices. Sloane's is loudest, then Bean's, Artie's, Lefty's, Louie's. And isn't it just like them, Chowder thinks, so impatient to get in those Death Keg punches. The whole house shakes when they march up the stairs, and Mrs. Ray is practically knocked down trying to block them from the bathroom. Instant mud as their sneakers touch the wet floor.

"Get outta my house, monsters! This is my house and I say get out!" She throws her head around and looks desperately at Chowder. It sounds like an exorcism.

But the five lifeguards, huge guys, make more noise breathing than she does yelling her head off. And in the bright, crowded bathroom, she's only a speck. Chowder, standing near her, can see directly into her scalp.

"It's cool, ma'am," says Sloane. "You ain't gotta worry, we're his friends."

"Outta my house," again, as if she doesn't know any other words. Her face, sweaty, pink, reminds Chowderhead of a little girl's.

"Look at it this way," Sloane beams, ready to explain. Something to check out. Sloane is known for only one tactic—brutality. Just how will he get around this?

"Look at it like, well, like a wake. Ya celebrate wakes even though you're sad, you gotta celebrate to like get through it. Otherwise, Christ, who knows—ulcers, heartburn, indigestion. You wouldn't want Timmy havin—"

"Wrong." From Louie. "Wakes are for dead people and Timmy's alive. I'd say it's more like a consolation prize."

"Don't be a jerk."

"I'm just sayin—"

"Well, someone's dead, else we wouldn't be here."

"Yeah, but—"

"Outta my house!" And on and on like that till everyone shuts up and stares at Timmy, it being suddenly apparent that there's no real excuse or reason for the Death Keg, it just *is*. Mrs. Ray sits on the toilet and cries.

"I wasn't gonna cop out, he'll be there," Chowder tells Sloane.

"We didn't give ya all night, we said nine and it's at least that now."

"I said don't worry, he'll be there. I was tied up."

"*I'll* fuckin tie you up." Sloane pushes him against the wall. The toothbrush rack trembles. "Who made you boss? You got special privileges we don't know about?" He punches at Chowder's chin. "What are youse, a coupla lovers?" Only Sloane can make a word like "lovers" sound completely disgusting.

Chowder is about to have it out, right here in the bathroom. But Timmy starts to clap and Chowder, assuming it's some kind of psychological warfare, joins in. Sure enough, Sloane backs off, confused.

Timmy's standing up, dripping, beginning to shout. He throws water around, not caring who he soaks.

"Does anyone ask me? Ya wanna know how psyched I am for this keg? I CAN'T WAIT! I been waitin all day, all my life! If anyone woulda asked me, I woulda said so, but no one asks me! I CAN'T FUCKING WAIT!"

Everyone is shocked. In that case, Sloane says, they'll leave. But they'll be back to drag him out if he doesn't show in half an hour. "Things might get messier than they need to." Then he yanks at his crotch, slaps Chowder across the head, bows to Mrs. Ray, and walks out. Bean, Artie, Lefty, and Louie the Lump trail single-file behind him.

They run with Timmy laid flat above their heads. Spin him around, around, throw him in the air. He hardly even touches their hands before bouncing back up again. Light as a kid. "DEATH KEG, DEATH KEG, DEATH KEG." Each firework shower blazing out of Playland doubles the frenzy, triples it, as if cues are somehow being given from up there. Their big faces, glowing, darkening, glowing again like a slow strobe. No moon anywhere, and you can almost believe there isn't one.

Moon's exploded, Alex half-thinks, along with everything else. Blown up and hurled in pieces, dissolving itself into the sand. She used to be frightened of firework noise, would cover her ears while her parents laughed, "Silly girl, it's a treat. Look at the pretty colors." Now the sounds she wants blocked are right here on the beach.

"DEATH KEG, DEATH KEG," stress on "death," "keg" barely a whisper. The only word these boys have ever cared to en-nunciate—"death"—like cheerleaders at some warped pep rally. It occurs to her that nothing with this much energy can last long before burning out.

Once Death Kegs were only ghost stories. Big kids on stoops talking in that soft way that meant they were letting you in on something. "My brother told me . . ." Then, later, she was the talker, bragging to out-of-town cousins and camp friends like no big deal, happens every day, proud of Rockaway for its gruesomeness.

And it'd come up sometimes in games of Truth or Dare. Invariably the person dared to crash a Death Keg would choose truth. The real truth is, Alex had never been. Had always gotten the impression it was bad etiquette to ask, faintly holy. And not flesh-blood-church holy either, but holy like a secret. Like the Indian rituals she'd read about at Camden that no outsider had ever seen.

It's like nothing she has ever seen when Sloane stops laughing, stops running, lets go of Timmy's head, lets it drop back, screams, "Shut up, maggots!" She huddles near Peg while old veteran guards who've come to reminisce nod like they know something, fill plastic cups. The guards fall into a slow procession around the fire. Timmy's head's still dangling.

"Murderer Ray, murderer Ray" around the fire, so softly, could be wind; so in step it looks rehearsed.

Sloane finds a piece of driftwood for a torch and wants everyone to have one. But Louie points out that they can't hold Timmy *and* the torches and there is no fuss about it. Sloane holds the flaming stick in front of Timmy's face and walks backwards.

"God, he must be sick," Peg says. "Moving around upside down, that awful face upside down."

"OPEN YOUR EYES, BOY!" yells Sloane. "WELCOME TO THE MURDERERS' CLUB!" Timmy tries spitting at him but misses completely, not even a graze.

"Thank God I'm a girl," Peg says, crossing her arms over her chest, though she's sweating. It's still hot. "That's one good thing."

"They'd do it to you," Alex says, just guessing.

"I know, but I don't haveta hold him up, I don't haveta strip and do the elephant walk."

Alex doesn't want to ask what *that* is. Peg's voice, always hoarse, sounds like static tonight. Alex notices she's wearing makeup, a skirt and makeup. She didn't know Peg owned that kind of stuff, and she looks so uncomfortable, having to hold the skirt down in the wind.

"No one's gonna force me to harass Timmy," she says. "I won't, I'll quit."

"No one's gonna force you to do anything," says Alex, not at all convincingly. She doesn't make any rules here. All she can do is hug Peg, and as she does she lets a mosquito suck blood from her wrist.

Timmy had scared her pretty bad. Out of his mind, arriving at the Keg in skeleton costume. Shovel in one hand, near-empty bottle of JD in the other. They'll be talking about it for years. Fucking hilarious—Mr. Murderer giggling and pointing his shovel at God. Oh God, it wasn't just the shovel either. Timmy's whole face looked different, locked into this one hard, crooked expression. "I'm ready! Let's go, boneheads, I'm ready!" Like it was just another road trip to the Jersey shore with the boys. And for some reason, Alex can't stop wondering where he got the costume.

She's heard all about Halloween, a hundred times she's heard it. Timmy dressing up not as a skeleton but as Geraldine Ferraro. How no one could guess who he was supposed to be but how some machismo Brooklynite tried to pick him up anyway. Timmy, playing along for a while as a goof, "showed that doof a coupla things."

The skeleton costume, made for a kid, is skin tight, almost obscene.

"X marks the spot, with a dot-dot-dot."

Timmy, set free for a moment while the fire's replenished, stands behind Alex, playing the children's game on her back. So eerie hearing *that*, out of nowhere. So eerie to hear he remembers every word of it.

"With a dash-dash-dash and a *biiiig* question mark."

It tickles where his fingers dot the question mark on her spine.

"Blood rushes up, blood rushes down, blood rushes all around."

"Timmy, what's going on?"

"With a pinch and a squeeze and a *cooool* ocean breeze." He pushes her hair aside to blow against her neck. The simulated ocean breeze feels good in the heat, but when she turns to say so they're pulling him away. Ordering him to dig a hole with his shovel, a vertical make-believe grave for himself.

It's Sloane's idea to dig close to the fire so Timmy'll keep "toasty," and to bury him facing the shack so he'll be able to see once the elephant walk starts.

Chowderhead says he has to take a piss and darts down to the shore. Wishing Peg would follow. Wishing it was tomorrow already.

The keg party, which is supposed to be *for* Timmy, seems to have turned into something against him. It can't be stopped. If Timmy hadn't screwed up and lost that kid, if Timmy had not ruined their perfect record, there'd be mass celebration; they'd all be called supermen. As it is, they're just overtired, mad, overheated, drunk, crazed, coked-up bad.

In the distance Chowder can hear a radio or a car or something and, more clearly, Sloane's dog, Schizo, howling in his whiny way at the cheap firecrackers. Bought, no doubt, from the Puerto Ricans who sell them out of car trunks to junior-high boys. Good for putting in bottles, for blowing your eyes out.

A kid they knew in grammar school, Chris Kegen, blew his eye out. Then he got in the habit of removing his glass eyeball at lunch. Forcing the empty socket on everyone, girls and nuns even. Kegen had the Death Keg spirit as a ten-year-old, and would fit right in here. But he's been in jail for a while now. Assault and battery after attacking his girlfriend's father with a can opener.

Chowder takes a long piss, aiming first at a corroded log that the tide keeps covering and uncovering, then shifting his hips to get the moving targets. Pretzel bags, tampon applicators, chewed-up wooden ice cream spoons, all sorts of shit blowing around in the heat. He'd pick it up to burn if the plastic stuff wouldn't smell so bad. There seems no point in picking up only some of the garbage and leaving the rest.

As he fastens the Velcro on his shorts, he watches Ambrose lighthouse pulse, and he imagines a stream of piss that could reach all the way out there, dampen the light easy as a candle. Not feeling drunk enough, he heads back up.

Earlier, after he left Timmy screaming in his bathtub, he'd gone to get Alex. She, of course, already knew, said that after work she had found Peg at home, cleaning the house. "You wouldn't believe how clean that house looked."

They talked about Peg for a long time. Then about how incredible it all was, fifteen lifeguards saving twenty-nine people and only one measly death. How much worse it could have been. How Rockaway would make the *Times*, TV, maybe the mayor'd even come down to thank them personally. Maybe it *was* the barge's fault, maybe it wasn't. All the while both of them thinking Poor Timmy. Thinking also about Sloane saving ten people and not even caring, just seeing how many he could save, some sort of endurance test. And shit, whatever anyone says, *it just isn't fair.*

On the way to the Keg, Alex wished on a star, but it was more like she was begging. "I wish I may, I wish I might, please, please, please, please have the wish I wish tonight." She said she always saw a lot of stars at once. That really it's impossible to see only one unless only one is there. Chowder asked who she thought she was kidding. It bugged him that she was doing this meaningless thing, but he also felt cruel for being bugged. He asked what she wished.

"You know," she said.

But he didn't.

When Chowder gets back to the top of the beach, Timmy is buried up to his neck and the boys are climbing on the shack roof, calling Chowder to get his ass up there for the elephant walk.

He tries to ignore them, goes and kneels by Timmy's head. It's real hot this close to the fire, and the wind keeps changing direction so embers fly toward them. Already there are three large welts on his friend's neck.

"You OK?"

"I think I'm gonna puke."

"I'll get the shovel and—"

"They'll kill you."

"But—"

"But nothing, get up there, fag."

Chowder runs to the keg for some ice but all the guards are getting antsy now. As if they can't stand the thought of walking in circles naked without him. They throw M80's off the roof—aiming? hooting, belching.

"Wouldya put some ice on Timmy's neck?" he asks Alex.

"What?"

"It's burnt." Chowder doesn't know why but suddenly the ice seems extremely important. He makes her promise.

"Well, sure, sure, of course."

Alex watches him take off his clothes as he walks toward the shack. She's seen lifeguards remove windbreakers, sweatpants in this same way as they've run to save swimmers. She feels an urge to follow him, gather his dropped clothing, hold on to it.

Peg says, "This is gonna sound weird but I really want to sleep with him again."

"Before or after he jumps off the bridge?"

"Before *or* after."

It's taking her a couple of minutes to go to Timmy. He looks so pathetic like that, just a head, and she tries persuading Peg to come with her.

"You know he only wants you," Peg says in the same teasing voice she uses to say "college girl," "bookbrain," "Campus Queen."

"You know we went out once, Cruise to Nowhere."

Alex doesn't know what she means. "You and Timmy?"

"Yeah."

Flashes of Peg talking to Joe, talking to Ponzio, Timmy,

Chowderhead. Then Peg as captain, always—kickball, punchball, softball—choosing Alex first for her team. And Peg choosing Timmy first, seven minutes in heaven in the showerhouse. How many minutes in hell to find the kid? Peg cleaning, cleaning the house till even her mother got worried. Had she meant that she wanted to sleep with Timmy? Had she done it already? And why all this now?

In her confusion, Alex is reminded of something a teacher once said. How in some places, or maybe one place, in Italy, the wind sends fish flying for miles out of the water. You can be walking through a field and find a fish.

That's her, out of place, in school, at home, out of things to say, hard to breathe, hard to understand anything about anything. When she leaves Peg standing there, hair all in her face, there's nothing left to feel except young and a little sad.

She wonders if Timmy is watching her walk toward him, if it's possible that he's smiling. But the firelight plays tricks, and with his pupils so big, with his hair matted to his forehead, neck, from sweat, it's unlikely.

"You must be dying."

"Dead and buried," he says in strange falsetto.

"I wish I knew what to say."

"I wish you knew what to say."

"Chowder told me to bring this ice."

"Smear it on my face."

"But I thought your neck got—"

"Smear it on my face."

So she does. Chowder has wrapped the ice in a T-shirt that says "No Guts, No Glory." She takes two cubes out and drops the shirt in the sand, then reaches down to the red wet face. As her hand passes his mouth, he licks it, and even though that seems peculiar she leans and kisses him. He's so eager it's scary, and his mouth, dry, tastes of JD, blood, sand. He bit his tongue, he says, when they pushed him in the hole.

"Can't I dig you out?"

"No."

"Just your arms?"

"Do that again."

"What?"

Chowderhead has to pretend he's enjoying himself. Already they don't trust him, and it won't help things any to get beat up. For now he'll just watch. Make sure they don't go too far. Not that he'd know what to do if they did, but something might come to him.

Bean's hairy ass in front of him. He hums along with the rest. They hum nothing in particular, nothing melodic, just a flat, insistent drone like cicadas in the fall when they're dying all over the sidewalks and on the tops of cars. He thinks how they probably all look more like apes than elephants. Hunched, swinging their shoulders, arms through their legs for trunks. And what elephants have to do with drowning anyway he cannot figure out.

If he looks down now, he'll see Timmy's head by the fire, maybe *on fire* by this point, who knows. But he can't look or else can't keep going around, around.

"They're goin in circles again. They're always goin in circles," says Alex to Timmy.

"I know."

"I wanna pray, is that stupid?"

"Yes."

When the boys get bored of the elephant walk they don't bother putting clothes back on. Alex watches them jump, all at the same time, off the trailer and into the sand. Their bodies are perfect, tan, with smooth swimmers' muscles, and from where she stands, unable to see their faces, just those bodies lit up by flashlight, she can't help thinking how beautiful they are. Like carved from some rare wood, not an excess piece anywhere. And though the attraction scares her, coming at this moment—how low—she's entranced. She cannot stop staring.

They disappear for a second, then come charging full speed toward her, toward Timmy. She wants to hide him. The guards laugh, cartwheel, some swing huge black pails. Peg races up, says, oddly, "My parents have these very same garbage pails." Then she looks at Timmy and starts to cry.

"Stop bawlin," he says. "What are you, a lady or somethin?" It sounds as if he might even have managed a smile this time, but Peg and Alex have been knocked away, can't see. Mounds of live jellyfish, sand crabs, and mud dumped in Timmy's hair.

When Alex realizes what has happened, it poisons her; she loses all control. Throws herself at Sloane, screaming "Fuckhead!," scratching, punching at his arms, rock hard.

Lefty pulls her away, pushes her down on the sand, and holds her there, squirming.

"The little woman's feisty? Huh?" Lust turns quickly to disgust and she struggles, kicks, wants to hurt him bad, so bad.

"Look, I don't got no problem beatin on girls if they deserve it, so cool it, Alex. I like you. I've always liked you." Stroking her thigh now. "You ain't Timmy's property no more," he says, then forces his mouth down on hers.

"Leave her alone," Peg whispers, jumping on him, pulling at his hair, "get offa her."

"You want some too? There's plenty to go around," he howls. Alex is sure she'll suffocate with the two of them wrestling across her stomach.

Peg puts up a good fight, but it's Chowder who performs

the miracle. All he has to do is say they need help digging Timmy out and Lefty lets go, just gets up and walks away like nothing ever happened.

Chowder wraps his arms around Peg, smooths her hair, tries to wipe the smeared makeup from her face.

"I can't believe this," Peg is saying. "I never saw any dead people before they went to the place to get fixed up. And her chest was so small, like the size of my—"

"You're beautiful," he tells her. "You're so beautiful." But then, looking over at Alex—shirt torn, working on standing—he says, "I didn't know you had it in ya. I had no idea."

"I bit him," says Alex.

They dig Timmy out and he whacks at the crabs on his neck. The crabs don't sting the way the jellys do or even nip much, but they're worse anyhow, crawling over the burns and over his scalp and, now that he's dug out, down his costume. They're dying in there from lack of oxygen.

He feels buried still. The way when you take a hat off you sometimes continue to feel it on your head. He's also so stiff and drunk and nervous that he jumps whenever a firecracker goes off. Artie hands him a beer, and he throws it right back in Artie's face. Grabs the shovel and starts to dig a second keg, underneath the sand.

But he doesn't believe it's a keg, has it in his head that a person is buried under there, that he has to get his person out before the person stops breathing. Timmy can hear him breathing.

They tackle him, drag him by one arm to the shore. "Wait, I gotta get him out, please, he's in trouble, please, I'm not kidding, oh no, not water, no water, *anything* else." Shells and broken glass cut him all the way down to the shore, and the shovel, still in his hand, makes a narrow path through the sand.

First dunk, it's panic. Legs won't move. Heart's gonna

burst. Then it fills his head, the man under the sand is him, under the water. By the third dunk, his body's relaxing; better, something clears. No, there is no man. Yes, he *can* swim. He gets an idea.

It's silent underwater. Nice. It'd be easy to just let go and stay there. At least, have them think he wants to. He makes himself limp, slips from the thick hands and swims, swims, dives to the bottom.

If he really had the balls to go through with it, it'd be only a few more minutes. It surprises him that his whole life doesn't flash before his eyes like they tell you. So he tries to make it. Only two images. Alex's face one time, watching smeared firefly parts glow on the bottom of his Pro-Keds. And his mother's face, in the backyard, as she concentrates on mosquitoes, lured, sizzled, in the purple bug light. That's it? Faces? Bugs? He tells himself that if he were serious about dying, there'd be more. And he thinks of heaven, which he still has faith in and which he's sure Agnes will get him into somehow.

As they pull him out, Timmy decides that God is chickenshit next to the ocean. He'll explain that to Alex, who wanted to pray, ha. Half his life praying had gotten him as far as the Murderers' Club.

THE BRASS BALLS | 14
BRIDGE JUMPERS
ASSOCIATION

The Brass Balls Bridge Jumpers Association would meet at two a.m. on the entrance ramp to the Gil Hodges Memorial Marine Park Bridge. It's one of the three bridges connecting Rockaway to other parts of Long Island—reserved for one night a year, this one, and though no one knows where the tradition began, there is a vague sense in everyone involved that jumping sixty feet into a swift, dark current and Independence Day have always and will always belong together.

For other times, for practice, there's the Cross Bay, built on top of an old wooden structure with vertical pilings that stick up or disappear, according to the tide, and on which Alicia McHenry's younger brother last year lethally impaled himself. Never even hit water, poor guy, just hung there, like a puppet.

The other, the Atlantic Beach, presents the danger of hitting bottom at low tide, drowning because your feet are stuck in the mud. But the bars on either side of Reynolds Channel, all within swimming distance of the thirty-foot bridge, easily keep it the favorite.

And after all, as Lefty likes to say, there's no better way in hell to get a girl than to tell her you just jumped off that bridge over there *for her*. Risked your life *for her* because you were too impatient to take a shortcut. Then, "I'm cold," "I may be hurt," sapping that ancient maternal instinct for all it's worth.

> X marks the spot
> With a dot-dot-dot
> With a dash-dash-dash
> And a *biiiig* question mark.
> Blood rushes up
> Blood rushes down
> Blood rushes all around.
> With a pinch and a squeeze
> And a *cooool* ocean breeze.

This time it's Alex playing, but she sings the rhyme instead of saying it, and brushes her finger against his back only when she makes the dots and X's.

Timmy never wants to move again. Hasn't moved since they first laid him here, crown of seaweed, how long ago? Sloane kicked sand so it sprayed. "Guess that's enough," he said, "welcome to the Murderers' Club," and he crossed himself for a finale. But the real finale would be at the bridge. No one had to say that, although Bean did, and had the nerve to add "Are you OK?" before Timmy blacked out.

Now everyone is gone, except of course Alex; except of course Chowderhead, who paces, says he won't jump; except of course Peg, who says she will. She's always wanted to; now she will. "What's the big deal? Sloane's not such hot shit, anyone can jump off a bridge, what's the big deal?" You can tell she's frustrated as she tries to light a joint in the wind.

Timmy reaches behind him and stops one of Alex's hands, holds it. It's real cold and sweaty at the same time. He rolls over to get the other one, puts both hands against his chest, not pulling her down on him as he'd like but imagining it. How her skin would feel, hot from sunburn.

Alex watches Timmy watch her. She's conscious of the tide getting closer, about to get them wet. Almost touching her shoe, then receding a little, nearer still, then receding. Like those karate exercises Lars does, seeing how close you can get to something without hitting it, or the lover game, how close without touching. Since Timmy's already wet there's no point in warning him. The way he looks reminds Alex of the TV people on the beach this afternoon and of another game they used to play. The Man Who Crawled Out of the Sea. Whoever's "it" gets to be the man who swam all the way from China and finally made it, half-dead by then, crawling out to a mob of kids (reporters) all talking at once and shoving empty bottles for mikes in his face.

"Tell me, Man Who Crawled Out of the Sea, what's it like? What did you eat? What did you think about? How long did it take you? Why did you do it and how's things in China? You're famous! You'll be in *The Guinness Book of World Records*, what's your name? We'll put you on TV. You're famous, we love you, Man Who Crawled Out of the Sea."

"Sleep," Chowder says as they walk toward the bridge. "If you'll go home and sleep, I'll do ya a favor and return the kegs."

"I *been* sleepin," Timmy says, and "Whataya mean I gotta return the kegs, what is this?"

"This is not a free country is what. Your Death Keg, your deposit."

"You should know *that*," Peg agrees.

They pass the giant bathhouse at Riis Park without saying anything. Timmy's legs feel like rubber bands and itch something wicked inside his costume. Caked in mud, dried bourbon, some blood, the skeleton disguise feels looser somehow. But in spite of himself Timmy smiles, because his arm around Alex's waist meets no objection and because their steps are in synch, left, right, left.

Alex smiles back, allowing his hand to stay, stray if it wants. It seems the only thing she can do for him. But her passivity is due mostly to pity, an emotion that depresses her, makes her smile all wrong. She knows he knows this. And she knows he still wants her anyway.

"Just what are you tryin to prove?" asks Chowder, still intent on talking Timmy out of it.

"It's got nothin to do with that," says Timmy. "Tradition's tradition—ya gotta, ya know, respect it."

"No, I don't know."

"Last year you knew, and the year before, and the year before. Gung ho! What's the difference?"

"The difference?" Chowder spits into a shrub. "I'm not as cool as I used to be, and even when I was, it was kicks, a thrill, you knew that. What's this tradition bullshit?"

Timmy is disillusioned. "Last year we sung 'My Country 'Tis of Thee' and jumped off together."

"Yeah, well, if you remember, last year I also gave myself a fuckin concussion."

And Alex points out there was also that jerk who jumped from a jetty last summer and broke his neck.

"That's different," Timmy says.

Chowder shakes and shakes his head. It's not different. It happened on *his* beach. For weeks afterwards, vegetables were placed in his locker as reminders. Now the things that once seemed daring or wild would never be fun again. The jetty incident had been only the beginning.

Approaching the bridge, they hear Schizo's high-pitched

yap and see Seaver, metal of his wheelchair glinting in the light. He'll ask Seaver to explain. That might work. Might.

It's Peg who Chowder really has to worry about. She won't stop asking questions.

"Howdaya do it? Dive or just jump?"

"Well," Chowder tells her, exasperated, "I don't know what kind of Olympic diving you been doing, but if you've never dove sixty feet, I'd suggest jumping, then I'd suggest praying."

He's intended to scare her by mentioning the height, but it seems only to have excited her more.

"Sixty feet! Wow!"

"Feels wonderful," Timmy says. "Feels like you've flung yourself offa the planet. No better way to go."

They all stare at him.

"I mean if I *had* to."

"Bunch of lunatics," says Chowder. "Tell her how it feels to hit. Pavement, darling."

"Pavement," Timmy confirms.

"Maybe I should drink more first," says Peg.

"Maybe you should kill yourself now and save time," says Alex.

Chowder tells them he'll murder the next person who mentions suicide and he walks toward Seaver. They all follow. Manhattan glitters across the bay, but the Coast Guard station at the base of the bridge is black.

"Don't tell me *he's* gonna jump," Alex says, looking at Seaver and at the same time wondering what it is that Schizo's so worked up about. She notices that Sloane is soaked, and figures he's already jumped because his skin's raw red. His efforts at shutting the dog up seem useless.

Seaver waves with a newspaper and everyone is sure it's a newspaper with something about *them* in it, but it turns out to be just the local paper and last week's at that. He probably found it in someone's garbage. He's wearing the Famous Bartenders School T-shirt and the sunglasses that Chowder gave him recently for a birthday present. Timmy, naturally, didn't believe it was really his birthday, but decided it had to be sooner or later and gave a bottle of 151 rum and a package of Fig Newtons. The presents had made Seaver blubber, and Chowder knew that he now wore the sunglasses even at night as a way of thanking him.

They slap his hands hello and Alex says, "Bet you're proud of Gooden's pitching." Which is extremely surprising. Since when does she know anything about baseball? Timmy could kiss her.

All attention turns toward Louie, who's standing on the railing, knees bent like it's an old diving board. "Hail, Mary, full of grace. The Lord is with thee. Blessed art thou amongst women. Blessed is the fruit of thy womb, Jesus. Holy Mary mother of God. Pray for us sinners now—"

Sloane slaps Timmy's back and offers him some brown liquid in a paper bag.

"Fuck yourself," Timmy says, then turns back to Louie. "Remember, man, land like a cat, land like a cat."

Which he may or may not have heard as he fell. Falling, his "A-MEN" getting tinier and tinier until it's stopped short. *Smack*, like a ball connecting well with a bat, Chowder says Seaver says.

Schizo's lost all control, barking down at the water, and Sloane's beating on him, "Quiet, mutt!" only bothering him more.

Alex finds herself worrying about Louie the Lump, imagine, she never even liked him. She leans over the rail with the rest until his head raises up. Faintly a splash. Faintly his yell up through the dark: "Yowee" or "Yahoo" or "Oh no," victory or pain, it's hard to tell from this distance, but it's something with energy and two syllables, that's for sure.

"Christ!" says Timmy. "He landed all wrong, lucky fuck. That musta killed." Alex is impressed he can tell.

Seaver is tugging at Timmy's sleeve and writing something to him in the margin of his newspaper. It's weird to see the guy with a pen. Where'd he get a pen? For some reason, Timmy has always assumed he didn't read or write.

And on top of it all, his handwriting is remarkably neat, with little curls at the ends of each letter. "How do you think I got" is all he can jot down before Chowder sees and freaks out, rips the pen from his hand.

"What's this? I can understand without *this!*" Chowder whips the pen into the bay. "Since when do ya need *this?*" He storms over to where Peg stands watching Louie climb out of the water and onto the rocks.

Seaver is pointing emphatically at his wheelchair.

"All right!" Timmy yells to Chowder. "Tell me then. If you're such a mind reader, tell me! 'How do you think I got'—what? You're so smart, tell me."

That's when it hits Alex. How Seaver got *there*, here, in his wheelchair. Oh, she has to think, but that damn dog won't stop barking and it's all so unreal. Seaver? Young as Timmy? Strong? With bright hair, standing right here, right where Louie stood and— She would not say anything. What if she's wrong? Seaver might get insulted, and that can't happen. She likes him. Everyone likes him because his face is cracked and kind.

She touches his shoulder and looks past it to the headlines in the paper. "Murphy Batting a Thousand," a typical *Wave* story. Man hears someone breaking into his house and stands ready with a bat to knock the intruder down a flight of stairs, unconscious. Yes, that's Rockaway's idea of a real hero. Enough to make her sick. But worse, there's the other type, exalted in an article on the very same page: "Carol McFey Ready to Serve Food," a graduate of Brooklyn College who got a job working for a food service.

"Who cares." She must have said it out loud, because Timmy gets all upset.

"I care! I wanna know what Seaver's got to say."

"No. That's not what I meant." Seaver is still pointing at his chair for Timmy's benefit, but Timmy is looking at Chowder instead, not even noticing.

"Just look at him if you wanna know so bad," screams Chowder, pissed. "Trust yourself for once." But Schizo drowns out the words as he welcomes Louie back. The Man Who Crawled Out of the Sea.

"Here I am, in the flesh," Louie says to no one in particular; then wincing, "I think I mighta broke somethin." He takes a towel off his bike, takes a seat, takes the brown paper bag from Sloane. "Doesn't your animal ever get hoarse?" he asks and laughs, clutching his side.

Sloane's fed up. He holds the wired dog over the water.

"You think you're a lifeguard, Schiz? You're gonna prove it. You think you're a man? Dog? What?" And before anyone can protest, Schizo's dropping sixty feet into nowhere.

"How could you do that?" Peg is pulling her shoes off, runs to the entrance ramp and leaps in, not a word. Then Chowder right in after her. Like dominoes, all three in the air at once, at different levels.

Gasps and "Holy shit" from everyone. Peg's skirt balloons up over her head, which is maybe why she's so silent, falling. Falling from half the height that Louie jumped, or Schizo, but it seems to take much longer, forever. Chowder's tremendous wail makes up for the worst of it.

She's dead, Timmy thinks. She's dead and Chowder'll crack his skull, and it'll all be my fault, again. Chowder thinks, She's dead and I'll crack my skull again, and it'll be all my fault. Alex doesn't think. Doesn't even breathe till she can see Peg again, then Chowder. Just heads; like Timmy had been, buried in the sand.

"Are you OK? You idiot! Are you OK?" she calls down, and although Peg doesn't answer she waves her arm, a good sign.

"Amazing," Bean says. "I'll marry her."

Louie complains that it hurts to breathe, his rib, something's wrong with his rib.

Seaver is shaking his head. His groans and gurgles sound to Alex like a tape deck whose batteries are shot or a forty-five record on thirty-three. And there's no time to try to decipher it now. Schizo, vanished. Timmy, about to jump. Peg, wrestling with Chowder in the bay.

From up on the rail, the water looks alive. It's breathing. Chowder is trying to pull Peg out but she won't have it. She can take care of herself. Timmy knows all about such things because it happens a lot, trying to save people from drowning on the beach. Some people would honestly rather drown than have to admit they were rescued.

Peg must have seen it even more times than he has since that type especially resents being saved by a woman. Still, she's doing the same thing, as stubborn as the many obscure saints Aunt Agnes used to whisper bedtime stories to him about. St. Gemma, refusing anesthesia when her diseased bone needed scraping. St. Julia, who allowed all her hair to be torn off. Worst of all, St. Thecla—she was a main character in dozens of Timmy's nightmares because she flung herself into pits (fire, serpents, wild beasts) and eventually died by being bound to bulls driven in different directions. It is not merely a question of proving yourself to death, you have to enjoy it.

Timmy, hoping he's different, assuring himself yes, he's

different, makes up his mind not to jump and already feels better. Because it has come to him. Without anyone having to tell him, it comes to him that Seaver crippled himself leaping from a bridge, this bridge maybe, twenty years ago maybe, for the same ridiculous reason. And bit his own fool tongue off.

It's the kind of story he'd never believe if someone else had told him, and it may not even be true, but for the first time Timmy sees how little that matters. The story makes sense; true or not, it still makes sense.

Peg and Chowder have gotten out of the water.

"Schizoooo!" Sloane moans. *"Schizoooo!"* so loud Timmy is positive the Coast Guard will drag themselves out of bed to see what the racket is. And that's all he needs now, when things have finally settled down—to be picked up by the Coast Guard again. Oh, his mother would surely kick him out for good then. No Good Timmy brings her nothing but trouble. No Good Timmy is driving her to that early grave whose tombstone she's already picked out and paid for. He wants to take Louie's bike, race home, and kiss her, promise to be good. Or take Alex's hand, race anywhere, and never go home again. But he gets off the rail and thanks Seaver instead. Kneels by the chair, with both his hands on the old guy's numb knees.

It's only when Seaver begins pulling apart the newspaper to wrap himself in it that Timmy feels strange, gets up and stands next to Alex.

"You know," "he whispers, "he's helpless. All we do is admire him and he's helpless."

"He's a good listener," Alex says. "And he can't gossip." Then, after a moment, "He never complains."

She wants to give Seaver her sweatshirt, but Timmy says no, goes and takes Sloane's. Sloane is in such a state over Schizo that he doesn't even notice.

Peg's back, in her arms a wet dead dog that no one's first aid can do a thing for.

"Schizo!" Sloane's eyes are actually wet. He takes the animal, lays it down on the ground and stares.

"I'm sorry, I swear I didn't mean it, oh God, Schiz, I'm sorry."

"Yeah, well, it's a little late for that, asshole," says Peg, her tone harsh at first but quickly softening, because, "Well, look at him," she tells Alex, "he's a mess." And what with his mother dead and his father in that detox place, she supposes he's getting his.

"But he's a hero," says Alex. "I saw him bragging on TV, tomorrow he'll be in all the papers. They're making him a lieutenant." She has this picture in her head. Sloane's picture, how it'll look in the papers; then Sloane himself thirty years from now, sitting in Duffy's and telling his story to anyone who'll listen. Skipping the dog part, naturally. Not forgetting, just leaving it out.

Louie's looking pale, so Chowder says he'll borrow his dad's car, take him to a hospital. Insists Peg come along, she's limping.

"I am not limping," Peg says, "but I'll keep you company. . . . Where are my shoes? Did I wear shoes?"

"Why'd ya do that?" Alex has to ask. " 'Cause of Schizo?" And she picks up Peg's sandals from the ground, by the railing.

Peg laughs, empty.

"Why'd I lose my virginity?" She looks at the sandals like they're someone else's. "Well, to see if I'd still be alive, of course." Then she allows Chowder to drag her away.

Timmy and Alex agree it is the longest day of their lives.

"Go home!" Chowder yells back at them. "Sleep!"

Artie and Lefty feel cheated. Party's over and they didn't get to jump. It's not too late; but with no one watching, what fun would it be? Impossible to drum up any interest—Bean passed out drunk, Timmy and Alex hugging, Seaver wheeling away. So they decide the hell with it, to carry Bean home and go hit the bars. Sloane, left alone on the bridge, nudges the cold thing with his toe. It just won't move.

July 6, 1987

Dear Sir, Dear Mr. Ray, Father, Dad,

Hello, hello out there. How are you?

I must have started this letter a billion times but this time I am also going to finish it. I don't have the paper, for one thing, or the patience or the brains to make it good. They taught us in high school, I think, but I still don't know and anyhow it wouldn't solve the problem of what to call you. I even thought of To Whom This May Concern. That was a joke, in a way.

But anyway, the important thing is that you keep reading (I might get to something) or that I keep writing (I might get to something). The important thing is that you don't freak out, thinking I'm going to come looking for you. I won't, ever, though of course I wanted to once. I saw this TV after-school special where all these adopted kids were trying to find their real parents and you know, I got it in my head. But Mom said it was just silly, I'm not even adopted, and thinking about it now I see that the program was really saying parents are the people that are nice to you or teach you something. Blood's beside the point.

So you might be glad to hear that other than Mom I've got this guy Seaver. Right now he's with me on the front steps, well, I'm on the steps and he's in his wheelchair. Mom doesn't like him, I can tell but as long as he's outside doesn't say so and even gives him food. Today that means soft brownish bananas and the oatmeal cookies nuns make to raise money for the church. It's all fine with me because it's nice and cool out here and every once in awhile we can see fireworks being lit off from the beach. Roman candles and bottle rockets mostly, nothing special but a lot of them. This Fourth everyone bought more fireworks than they knew what to do with. I don't know why. Across the street old man Corning is listening to the Beatles on his porch. It's funny. Everything seems OK tonight, but I think that has a lot to do with this letter. Letters help.

I used to have this girl to write to but now she's in town for the summer and when I was younger I wrote to companies and stuff, entering contests. In fifth grade I wrote to the Razzles company and won this essay thing. Is it a gum or is it a candy? All I said was that it was a stupid question. It's got to be gum because it ends up as gum so it's gum and they sent me twenty-five dollars and a whole lot of Razzles. But none of this is what I meant to say at all. I used to keep a journal. I thought maybe you'd come back and want to know what went on and I was afraid I wouldn't remember it right. But that was a long time ago too and now I'm not even sure where I put it.

I guess I'm curious. What do you do? What do you like, eat, think about? Since I've got nothing to go by I figure there's a good chance your name's Timothy too and I picture you as me but older on a ranch. The ranch is the one thing I do know but being twenty years ago, I might have to xerox this letter a billion times for the billion Rays in Ohio and it still may never get to you. But that's OK too because if I really believed you'd be reading this I couldn't just babble on like I am. If that makes sense.

Do you ever wonder about me? I want, I'm going to be a fireman. Now I'm a lifeguard. I like to party, surf, drive. I like the way girls with long hair have wet spots on the backs of their T-shirts after swimming. I like bugs. A lot. I seem to get into trouble a lot, which Mom blames on dropping out of high school, not going to confession, drinking.

I like to think you'd think different. Not worry so much about my soul. But that part's Agnes's fault. It rubs off.

Did you know Agnes? Were the two of them always this way? It's too bad about Agnes especially. She gives nuns a bad name when most of them are nice enough. Once she loses her temper she's the same as any old drunk in a bar, picking fights. And it's the same as my lifeguarding partner, Sloane. If he was the only lifeguard you ever met you'd think they were all mean. Crazy mean. I guess there's people like that wherever you look and I guess they'll all go to hell, except maybe Agnes, but it's hard remembering that sometimes.

Sometimes, I get the feeling that Mom, Agnes, a

lot of people think a good Christian isn't ever supposed to be happy or lucky and especially ever rich. They figure heaven's the real jackpot.

When the Lotto prize went up to forty-one million dollars, Mom wouldn't even buy a ticket. She said because she was afraid she'd win! It's weird but I think she can't wait to die and start enjoying herself. It makes me mad and sometimes I get cruel, start teasing her about immaculate conception.

Really, I know how it feels to be that into something because the way she is about God is the exact same way I am about this girl. Only the girl, she's solid. I may not always be able to touch her but I can be sure she'll stay solid. Do you know what I mean?

I read once about how mayfly worms live in the mud, in the bottom of a pond for eighteen years and how when they get out, finally become flies they mate and die all in an hour. That's living, huh? Well, don't feel like you have to write but

Take care,

Love,
Timmy

P.S. I'm sending along this picture that someone took last summer on a deep sea fishing boat. The guy on the left is my good friend Chowderhead and the other one, holding up the big fluke, that's me.

About the Author

Jill Eisenstadt was born and raised in Far Rockaway, New York. She was educated at Bennington College and Columbia University. She lives in New York City.

V I N T A G E
CONTEMPORARIES

"Today's novels for the readers of today."— V A N I T Y F A I R

"Real literature—originals and important reprints—in attractive, inexpensive paperbacks."— T H E L O S A N G E L E S T I M E S

"Prestigious."— T H E C H I C A G O T R I B U N E

"A very fine collection."— T H E C H R I S T I A N S C I E N C E M O N I T O R

"Adventurous and worthy."— S A T U R D A Y R E V I E W

"If you want to know what's on the cutting edge of American fiction, then these are the books you should be reading."
— U N I T E D P R E S S I N T E R N A T I O N A L

On sale at bookstores everywhere, but if otherwise unavailable, may be ordered from us. You can use this coupon, or phone (800) 638-6460.

Please send me the Vintage Contemporaries books I have checked on the reverse. I am enclosing $ _____ (add $1.00 per copy to cover postage and handling). Send check or money order—no cash or CODs, please. Prices are subject to change without notice.

NAME _____

ADDRESS _____

CITY _____ STATE _____ ZIP _____

Send coupons to:
RANDOM HOUSE, INC., 400 Hahn Road, Westminster, MD 21157
ATTN: ORDER ENTRY DEPARTMENT
Allow at least 4 weeks for delivery.

VINTAGE
CONTEMPORARIES